"This is probably the longest personal conversation we've ever had. Did you come all this way for *that*?" Eve asked.

"No."

"What then?" Her voice became a ghost of itself.

The indent at the corner of his lips deepened with humor.

"Oh, *don't*." Her breath shortened. All of her nerve pathways contracted with anticipation.

"I don't know what *you're* thinking," Dom mocked. "But I came to propose we marry."

If the entire mountainside had fallen down upon her, she couldn't have been more caught off guard.

"We can't. Why would you even want to?" Did he have feelings for her after all? That thought sent her own thoughts scattering. Her heart tripped and thumped, trying to take flight. Adrenaline zinged through her system, urging her to flee because she didn't want to have this conversation. She didn't want to examine how *she* felt about *him*.

"The feud doesn't serve anyone. It has to end," he said simply.

Canadian **Dani Collins** knew in high school that she wanted to write romance for a living. Twenty-five years later, after marrying her high school sweetheart, having two kids with him, working at several generic office jobs and submitting countless manuscripts, she got The Call. Her first Harlequin novel won the Reviewers' Choice Award for Best First in Series from *RT Book Reviews*. She now works in her own office, writing romance.

Books by Dani Collins

Harlequin Presents

Innocent in Her Enemy's Bed
Awakened on Her Royal Wedding Night

Four Weddings and a Baby

Cinderella's Secret Baby
Wedding Night with the Wrong Billionaire
A Convenient Ring to Claim Her
A Baby to Make Her His Bride

Bound by a Surrogate Baby

The Baby His Secretary Carries
The Secret of Their Billion-Dollar Baby

Diamonds of the Rich and Famous

Her Billion-Dollar Bump

Visit the Author Profile page
at Harlequin.com for more titles.

MARRYING THE ENEMY

DANI COLLINS

Harlequin

PRESENTS

Harlequin® PRESENTS™

ISBN-13: 978-1-335-93912-8

Marrying the Enemy

Copyright © 2024 by Dani Collins

Recycling programs for this product may not exist in your area.

For questions and comments about the quality of this book, please contact us at CustomerService@Harlequin.com.

TM and ® are trademarks of Harlequin Enterprises ULC.

Harlequin Enterprises ULC
22 Adelaide St. West, 41st Floor
Toronto, Ontario M5H 4E3, Canada
www.Harlequin.com

Printed in Lithuania

MIX
Paper | Supporting responsible forestry
FSC® C021394

MARRYING THE ENEMY

To my editor Laurie, who called this one her new favorite. Thank you for being so wonderful to work with. <3

CHAPTER ONE

Five years ago...

EVELINA VISCONTI PICKED up a text from her middle brother asking which club she and her friends were visiting tonight.

She texted back.

Tell Mom I'll call her tomorrow.

Their mother would have called him the second Eve refused to pick up her call, texting instead that she was out for the night.

Seconds later, her friend, Hailey, looked up from her own phone.

"Your brother wants to know which club we're at. He wants to drive down from Naples to join us. Should I tell him we're actually in Budapest?"

"No," Eve said with beleaguered annoyance. Why was her family *like* this?

Eve was twenty-one, celebrating the end of her university years and the beginning of life as an adult, not that any of her family saw her as such. It wasn't as though she had a history of getting into trouble, either. She'd been determined to prove herself academically so her partying had been confined to inviting friends onto her parents' yacht between semesters. Drinking a glass of wine during reading break was her version of bacchanalian excess.

When she had finished her latest exams, these friends from boarding school had urged her to come to the Amalfi Coast with them. Hours after arrival, Hailey had coaxed her uncle into flying them to Budapest for a pub crawl through the ruin bars.

Eve's mother had been chilly about her coming as far as the Amalfi Coast, having planned an introduction between Eve and her future husband. Or, a contender at least.

Allowing Eve to finish her degree before marrying her off had been an exercise in patience for Ginny Visconti, an American heiress herself. Ginny had been matched by her own mother in a very advantageous and comfortable arrangement when she was nineteen. If she or Eve's father had ever cheated, they'd hidden it well, but they weren't soulmates. They were partners in the business of securing and advancing Visconti Group, primarily a hotel and resort conglomerate with holdings and interests in related industries. Ginny had done her part by producing three sons, one every two years, before she closed up shop. A girl arrived unexpectedly, seven years later.

In many ways, Eve had been the overprotected, spoiled baby, always trying to catch up to her much older brothers. Her mother had discouraged her from horseplay and other tomboyish activities, constantly putting her in dresses and insisting she "act like a lady." The very second that Eve grew breasts, her mother had begun talking about her prospects and seeing her "settled."

Eve's entire purpose for existing seemed to revolve around the link she would forge between the Visconti dynasty and one of their cohort families. The fact her mother was going so far as to try sending her brother to chaperone her, to ensure her plan stayed on track, provoked a massive case of delayed adolescent rebellion in Eve.

She texted her brother.

Leave my friends alone. I'll fly back to New York Monday.

She turned off notifications and tucked her phone into the wallet that hung from a cross-body shoulder strap and let it drop against her hip.

"Isn't it time to go dancing?" she asked.

Everyone nodded. They'd started their evening in a quaint garden café for dinner, then made their way to a billiards bar to enjoy a cocktail. They had listened to a band for an hour in another outdoor bar and now headed into a stone factory built in the late eighteen hundreds. It was renowned for being converted into a labyrinth of bars, music venues and dance floors.

"If you decide to leave with someone, text the rest of us, yeah?" Hailey said, then tucked her chin to add playfully, "But assume that's what I've done. I'll see you sluts on the walk of shame tomorrow."

Everyone laughed, but Eve only smiled weakly. She didn't know *how* to hook up and had never really aspired to. She occasionally dated—mostly men her mother threw at her—and had kissed far too many toads, but she hadn't found anyone who tempted her into a long-term relationship, let alone his bed. Besides, her mother expected her to remain a virgin until she married, which Eve knew was grossly outdated, but she had been busy with her double major in marketing and hospitality management so that's exactly what she was.

Her lack of sexual experience made her feel like a terrific spinster against her friends. They were all sending speculative looks around the crowd as they entered the first bar, where a heartbeat of syncopated electronica seemed to pulse from the stone walls. Flashing lights rotated to spill color across the bouncing bodies on the floor.

Eve skipped ordering a drink. She loved good wine or a tangy, refreshing cocktail on a hot day, but she didn't enjoy feeling drugged or the cotton-headed nausea of a hangover so she always paced herself.

"Are you still playing dorm mother?" one of her friends teased.

Eve laughed off the remark and began to sway her hips as she moved onto the dance floor. She genuinely loved dancing and stayed there for several songs before breathlessly visiting the bar for a sparkling water.

A boisterous noise drew her attention as she moved to the end of the bar where she could watch the dancing.

A group of young men were coming in, a bachelor party, judging by the plastic shackle on one man's ankle. The chain was long enough to drape over his arm and the ball must have been full of alcohol because he brought it to his mouth and popped open a cap like a water bottle to pour something into his mouth, eliciting approval from his friends.

Their antics reminded her of her brothers except *that* one was different.

A visceral tugging sensation accosted the pit of her belly as she studied the one who wasn't laughing. He was older than the rest, close to thirty, and definitely came from money.

They all did, she noted with another brief glance at tailored cargo shorts and T-shirts with discreet designer logos. The mystery man was also casually dressed, but in sophisticated linen trousers that were barely creased. His short-sleeved button-down exposed beautiful biceps and a watch that she suspected was a Cartier Tank.

His cheeks wore a well-groomed stubble, his dark hair was combed back off his forehead and his straight brows suggested he was a man who never compromised. His mouth was unsmiling. Unamused.

He looked bored. *So* bored.

Which made her chuckle around the straw she had tucked between her teeth.

At that second, his gaze seemed to laser through the flashing lights and burn into her.

A fresh punch of intrigue tightened her abdomen, but she actually glanced behind herself, thinking *Me? No*.

The man said something to his companions and began winding his way toward her.

The tempo of her heartbeat increased, matching the music so closely, she felt as though she *became* music.

At the last second, he veered into the bar and waved a credit card, leaning in to place his order.

Well. Wasn't she full of herself? Apparently, her friends had lied when they had said this hot-pink halter top and sequined silver miniskirt were sexy on her. She wasn't the curviest figure in the room, though. She tended to run miles when she was stressed and, having just finished exams, was lean as a greyhound. Her mother was always trying to push her into padded bras, "for a more attractive silhouette," but Eve preferred to go without a bra altogether. In that way, she was happy to be less Marilyn Monroe, more ironing board.

"Are you alone?"

Her nerves leapt then froze, as though a panther had snuck up on her and took a curious, abrasive lick of her arm.

Mr. Tall, Dark and Disinterested was suddenly right beside her, leaning close so he didn't have to yell. His voice was like dark chocolate, too deep and earthy to be sweet, but enticing all the same.

She choked slightly at how close he was and covered her mouth, shaking her head.

"With friends." Her voice was so strained he had to read her lips. The sting of his stare made them tingle. She pointed to the dance floor, but there was no way he could tell who she meant.

Was that his aftershave that closed around her like an embrace? It was a delicious mingle of nutmeg and carnation, cedar and citrus, bergamot and black pepper. His aura of power was even more overwhelming, enveloping her in an energy field that paralyzed her body, yet left her nerve endings humming.

She wanted to touch him. That's all she could think as she skimmed her gaze across his chest and fixated on what looked like an ancient gold coin in the hollow of his throat.

"How old are you?" He sounded American, like her.

Affronted that he suspected she was underage, she said pithily, "Almost twenty-two."

"So twenty-one." His mouth quirked, equally pithy as he withdrew slightly.

"How old are you?" she challenged, instantly wanting him back into her space, even though it was like standing in the blast of a furnace.

"Almost too old for twenty-one." He turned to gather up the full tray of shots he'd ordered and balanced it easily on one hand. He paused long enough to offer her one, taking one for himself. "I'm Dom."

She bet he was a Dom. She'd read enough erotic romance to easily picture him as the sort who liked to control everything, especially sex. A sensual shiver worked its way from her nape to her navel.

"Eve." She took a drink off the full tray.

They shot their shots, he nodded, then took the tray to his friends.

She breathed through the fiery burn in her chest, left her empty glass on the bar, then rejoined her friends to continue dancing.

She didn't look to see where Dom had gone, but she knew exactly where he was. Through the next hours, as their two parties moved through the various tunnels and bars and clubs, down to the cellar and up to the terrace, she was always aware of him. Not because his group was big and rowdy, which they were, but because she could feel him. She knew when he was at the bar, or left the room, or was approached by a woman to dance. It was as though an invisible signal pulsed inside her, connecting her to him.

At one point, when she was in the ladies' room, her friend said, "My sister used to date one of those guys in that bachelor party."

"Which one?" Eve asked with a sharp pinch of jealousy.

"The sloppy one. That's why they're no longer dating. You go ahead," she added to Eve as she slid a flirty look to the woman who came to the sink.

Far be it from Eve to block anyone's good time. They'd already lost Hailey to a German fellow wearing skinny jeans and a tongue pierce. All her friends seemed to be finding a romantic partner except her.

Literally everyone was, Eve thought with amusement, as she left the washroom and passed an alcove where a couple was doing their best to have sex against a wall.

She was about to enter the club again when a drunken man lurched toward her.

She dodged him, thinking he was merely staggering, but he caught her around the waist from behind and tried to pull her into him. He slurred something in a language she didn't catch.

Reacting purely on instinct, Eve shifted her hips to the side so she could give his crotch a hard slap. As he choked out a pained, "Oof!" and released her, she spun to clip him on the ear.

She left him slumping to the floor against the wall and practically walked into another man. She pulled back her arm, ready to deliver a solid punch.

Dom closed his hand over her fist and leaned in. "Nice work."

Her adrenaline spiked anew, flooding her with the thrill of his touch and the proximity of his lips to her jaw.

"I have brothers." Just because her mother had discouraged her from wrestling with them didn't mean they hadn't taught her to "go for the groin" and protect herself.

"Come dance with me." Dom brought her hand down and slid his fingers between hers, leading her onto the dance floor.

She had already surreptitiously watched him move, mesmerized by the way he rolled his hips and rocked his wide shoulders. He had the grace of an athlete, every move smooth and perfectly timed.

For a moment, she felt off-beat and self-conscious, then his gaze slithered down her like a spell. Her body began to match him move for move, even though they weren't touching. He seemed completely focused on her, but she realized after a few moments that he was putting himself between her and other men, subtly turning her away from them or inserting himself, forcing them to keep their distance.

It was possessive and weirdly exciting, feeding the sizzle in her belly. She felt free to be as sexy as she wanted and looked him right in the eye as she set her foot between his and brushed up against him, then turned so her backside was nearly in his lap.

She barely touched him, but the hum inside her was a scream of anticipation. His wide palms held her hips as they began to grind together. His chest was against her back, his body caging hers.

This was how he would make love to her. Like an animal.

Arousal exploded through her at the thought. She saw, for the first time in her life, the raw appeal of sex. She wanted to be covered and held safe while he filled her and made her his. She wanted that so badly, she thrust her buttocks deeper into his fly, rubbing against the hardness there. Inviting more.

His touch firmed on her hips, pressing her to his erection before he released her and spun her to face him, then clasped her close. The sudden impact with his chest punched her breath from her lungs. His thighs were hard against hers, the ridge of his erection against her stomach, filling her mind with crude fantasies. She could feel those muscled legs pushing hers open. His weight would crush her pelvis while his mouth came down on hers—

He spun her away, catching her hand and twirling her.

She stood in flames, licked and lashed by the heat of his lust-filled gaze.

He brought her back against him, bending his knees so they were pelvis to pelvis. She had never been so aware of her own sex. Had never felt such an ache there, like a signal pulsing between her thighs, yearning for that thick shape that rubbed with such promise.

Connect. Join. *Mate.*

His teeth caught her earlobe, scraping lightly before he growled, "I have to keep my cousin's groom from drinking himself to death. Be good."

His mouth dipped into her neck and his arms tightened to hold her still while he marked her with a small hickey. He left her swaying in the crowd of strangers.

Be good? *Shut up.* She was tired of being good.

She was gone.

Domenico Blackwood took it like a chest punch when he could no longer see the midnight hair that picked up the purple hues of the flashing lights. The clock and his inner radar told him she was gone, likely with someone who would exploit the blatant sexuality she had pushed so tantalizingly into his lap.

He cursed, still aroused from the feel of her, and now he had a pool of tarlike anger in his belly.

She was too young for him, he reminded himself. She was a doe-eyed twenty-one to his jaded twenty-nine and he was a man with "a cold, empty heart." According to his ex-fiancée, at least. And popular opinion, no doubt.

At first glance, Eve and her squad had reminded him of the woman who'd broken off his engagement a few months ago. They might be party girls slumming with backpackers for a night of dancing, but their rich girl roots were as clear as the daddy-bought diamond studs in their ears.

Dom was more than ready for a rebound affair, but cold heart or not, he had promised his aunt on his mother's side that he'd ensure her soon-to-be son-in-law didn't do anything to ruin the extravagant wedding she'd spent a year planning.

The role of big brother to a bunch of drunks was painful, but at least Dom had had the eye candy of legs that went on for days. Eve's breasts were pretty teacups he craved to sip and her hair was long enough to wrap around his fist two or three times. The sparkle off her skirt as she'd swayed her hips gripped him like a hypnotist's pocket watch every time they crossed paths, moving in and out of the various bars and dance clubs.

When he'd glimpsed her heading to the ladies' room an hour ago, he had lingered to watch her come back, then grew concerned when he saw a swaggering club goer headed into the same tunnel.

By the time he got there to ensure she was all right, she was dusting her hands. Dom had been so turned on, he had wanted to press her to the wall and test the limits of public decency.

Asking her to dance was as much dereliction of duty as he allowed himself—and it was pure, erotic torture. She had natural rhythm and undeniable sensuality. When she had boldly looked into his eyes and rubbed up against him, he'd caught the fragrance of anise and lilac and the tang of her sweaty night. He wanted that smell all over him.

He had wanted her badly enough in those moments to recognize the danger she posed. He'd proposed to his fiancée specifically because she didn't get under his skin. He'd had a front row seat to a man consumed by his own emotions—two, in fact. His memories of his grandfather were dim, but they were similar, chilly recollections of a man haunted by a desire to settle a score. His father had been driven by the same crusade of anger, his grudges wearing away any softness in his soul, leaving only the hard, gnarled center.

Growing up in that fugue of antipathy had taught Dom to tamp down, bottle up and otherwise ignore his own feelings, lest they twist him into a similar, embittered version of himself. He never allowed anyone to needle him past his own control so, when Eve's lissome figure and alluring gaze had tempted him to forget his responsibilities, he'd made himself walk away with only that tiny taste of her against his lips.

There was nothing satisfying in being so noble, especially when he finally poured his future cousin into his hotel bed and went to his own in the penthouse. Dom had every kind of shower, trying to douse the hunger gnawing at him, but still only tossed and turned.

When he couldn't stand it any longer, he rose and dressed for a grueling, early-morning workout, planning to punish this craving out of himself, if that's what it took.

The fitness room wouldn't be open yet, but he owned the hotel. He owned the whole chain, in fact, along with the corporation that oversaw dozens of similar resorts and developments around the world. His card was all access, all the time.

When the elevator stopped midway down, he expected a family with young children to join him. Or a businessperson hurrying out for an early flight.

It was her. Eve. She wore a pair of shorts and a bright yellow windbreaker and a look of exactly as much surprise as gripped him. His sister would call this kismet. He didn't believe in such things. For him, it was merely coincidence. A convenient opportunity.

The hunter inside him leapt on it.

CHAPTER TWO

WHEN HER LAST friend had paired up with a woman wearing bright blue lipstick and an armful of bangles, Eve had caught a rideshare back to the hotel—which was the *real* crime she was committing here in Budapest. If her family knew she was staying in a WBE hotel, they would drag her out by the hair.

Eve hadn't realized where they were booked until they arrived. Hailey's uncle had paid for everything as a graduation gift to his niece. As their guest, Eve hadn't wanted to make a fuss so here she was, waking alone in a mini-suite that was as luxurious as any of the Visconti hotels.

She hadn't really slept. She blamed the alcohol and Hailey not coming back, but she knew what the real issue was. Dom had left her in a state of arousal that kept her fantasizing about a kiss she hadn't received. She had spent the restless hours imagining he had brought her back to this hotel and did more than kiss her.

At six thirty, when the sun came up and other early-morning joggers had started to emerge on the streets below, she dressed for a run.

She was skimming through her playlists as she

waited for the elevator when the doors opened to reveal *him*. Dom.

A jolt of electricity gripped her, freezing her in place.

"Are you just getting home?" she asked, even though
he wore gym shorts, sneakers and a plain blue T-shirt.

He shot out a hand to hold the door. "I can't sleep."
His growled voice seemed to blame her for that, which
sent a flutter of smug pleasure into her chest.

A wispy scent of risk stung her nostrils, though, even
as anticipation teased her stomach. She had cursed herself for not speaking to him before she left, not that she
knew how to invite a man to her room. The carefree
come-hither woman she'd been a few hours ago was
long gone, leaving a tongue-tied virgin who was blush-
ing over the thoughts she'd been thinking all night.

"Do you have your own room?" he asked in that same
gritty, intent tone.

Or he could just invite himself, she thought with mild
hysteria. The churn of nervous excitement increased in
her abdomen. Be good? Or…?

"My roommate isn't back yet." She tried to project
a sophistication she didn't possess. "Would you like to
see it?"

"I would." He stepped out, seeming bigger in daylight
than he had at the club. More intimidating.

He'd showered off the sweat of the club, but hadn't
shaved. The edges of his beard were scruffy, his eyes
alert, but sunken into the dark circles of a sleepless
night.

He nodded in a command for her to lead the way.

Her blood turned to champagne, bubbling and fizzing

as she walked, making her feel lightheaded. She wished that she was wearing her club clothes, not this bust-flattening sports bra and baggy shorts with a wind-breaker colored for visibility, not flattery.

Nervously, she let him into the sitting room. The pair of queen beds was visible through the open double doors to the bedroom. Hailey's bed was untouched, the other was tousled, revealing her fitful sleep.

She waved in a lame *Here it is* gesture. She had opened the drapes when she rose. The view of the river and the historic architecture on the far side was beau-tiful.

"It's great," he said, not taking his eyes off her. "Do you have condoms?"

Wow. She held his stare and swallowed the heart that had risen into her throat.

She could have demurred and told him he was moving too fast, but he wasn't. That was the weirdest thing. In any other case, such earthy bluntness would turn her off, but something more intuitive inside her was responding to his wavelength. She liked knowing he was feeling exactly as urgent as she did. It flooded her with erotic heat and more yearning than she could stand.

"Yes," she replied, because Hailey had made sure she knew there were some in the nightstand if she needed them.

"Do you want to show me where they are?" He sounded as though he was being deliberately careful and neutral, not sarcastic. Perhaps he realized how ag-gressive he was sounding and wanted to give her an op-portunity for second thoughts.

All she had to say was "no." She could easily tell him she'd rather go on her run and would see him at breakfast. She could open the door and say nothing at all. Her hand was still on the latch.

But her fingers were twitching to explore his smooth arms and she wanted to nuzzle her nose into his throat. Her lips were still dying for the press of his and the rest of her... The rest of her really, really wanted to know how his naked body would feel against hers. How his erection would feel inside her.

Her knees felt wobbly as she walked into the bedroom and opened the nightstand to take out the box. She set it beside the base of the lamp then kept her back to him, struck by bashfulness.

His weighty steps were silent on the thick carpet, but she felt his energy like a force as he arrived behind her. The heat of his body pressed like a physical touch against her back.

"What are you wearing under that?" His voice was a velvety caress in and of itself.

She turned and started to lift her hands to the zip, intending to show him, but realized she was still holding her phone. She tossed it onto her unmade bed and took hold of her collar with one hand, then slowly, slowly, drew her zip down.

He watched the descent of the tab the way a cat gave its single-minded attention to an unsuspecting prey, but his chin dipped in the smallest nod of approval as she let the jacket fall open to reveal her mauve bra.

"Sexy, right?" she said of its flattening fit.

"Very," he said in a low rumble.

He stepped closer and touched her chin. She thought he was going to kiss her, but his gaze slid to her throat. A faint smile eased the line of his stern mouth. He trailed his fingertip down to where he'd left the barely-there shadow of a love bite.

"I want to cover you with those." His voice was raspy from his late night and something else. Want?

"Maybe I'll do the same to you," she suggested boldly.

"Be my guest." He took hold of the open edges of her jacket and drew her into him.

She instinctively brought her hands up, but they only landed on the satin smoothness of his bare upper arms.

"You drove me crazy all night, Evie." He released her jacket and his wide hands slid inside to splay against her bare waist.

She gasped at his hot, possessive touch. Her skin tightened and tingled while her brain short-circuited over the way he had turned her name into an endearment.

"All I could think about was having your long legs around my waist. Around my neck."

Oh, that was dirty. Why did she find it so titillating? A helpless sob thrummed in her throat.

"My roommate might come back," she warned, voice as abraded as his.

"Does that turn you on?" He traced tickling patterns in her lower back that made her squirm in reaction and press closer to him in an attempt to escape it. "That we might get caught?"

"No." Yes. A little. Her senses were being bombarded by a lot right now. The heat and hardness and scent of him. The touch that was both light and merciless at the same time. A sense of anticipation and wonder and nervousness of the unknown.

"Do you want to lock the bedroom door?" he asked.

She should, but his hands were sliding into her shorts at the back, pushing them off her butt cheeks along with her underwear, leaving her backside bare to the cool room and the exploring massage of his hot palms.

It was incredibly disconcerting. She felt vulnerable and wicked and turned on. His roaming, claiming touch incited her to the point she could hardly speak, let alone move to do something so practical as…

"I want you to kiss me," she confessed in an aching whisper.

His reaction was a noise of approval and a firming of his hands on her ass. He dipped his head to capture her lips with his own.

This man knew how to kiss. Maybe there would have been a gentler preamble if they hadn't spent last night priming themselves for this moment, but he slicked his tongue between her lips, creating a damp seal that allowed him to consume her then he *did*.

Helplessly, she swept her arms up to cling around his neck, arching into him so she could find and feel his erection again. His hands on her backside pressed her mons firmly into that implacable ridge while he hungrily rocked his mouth against her own.

This was what she had wanted last night. What she had always wanted. Passionate oblivion. He was strong and sure and she instinctually knew he would keep her safe while absolutely ravishing her. She rubbed blatantly against him, stoking the heat that was gathering in her loins, seeking pressure against the knot of nerves that was swollen with every libidinous thought she'd had of him and a thousand new ones.

"I want that, too," he said, holding her hips tight to his as he lifted his head.

She was panting, so disoriented she wondered if she'd spoken her thoughts aloud, but she couldn't have. Her mouth had been occupied.

He kept her hips braced in his wide hands and ground his erection against her, making her eyelids flutter.

This was a perilous moment, she realized with muted alarm. Not because he seemed to be violent or cruel, but the way he drew her so effortlessly into acting without inhibition was sobering. She liked to believe she was a strong, confident, independent woman, but this stranger was using her own sensuality to undermine her sense and willpower.

He proved it by casually skimming her shorts down her legs, taking her underwear with them.

She gasped in surprise, but her only struggle was the fight to get her shod feet free. She should have unlaced and removed her shoes, but he was peeling his shirt over his head and catching her close again.

A small cry escaped her. The heat of him! He was tensile muscle and silky hair and slow, wicked hands as he guided her to rub her near-naked chest against his. She moaned, reveling in the brush of skin on skin, not realizing he was easing her onto the bed because it happened so effortlessly. She was too enthralled with mapping his back with her fingertips and using her inner thigh to caress his leg. His arm was a hard band around her, his other hand feathered touches behind her thigh and into the heat between.

His knee went onto the mattress as the cool bottom sheet arrived against her back. He stretched out alongside her, bracing on an elbow as he pushed her bra up to reveal her breasts.

"I want to tangle you up in this thing and have my way with you. Would you like that?" He caught the arm that was between them and tucked it under her lower back. The position arched her breasts up to him while lightly trapping her. He bent to lick at her pouted nipple, making it contract into a taut, sensitized peak.

"You're a little bit kinky, aren't you?" she accused breathlessly, turned on but also overwhelmed by his casual control. She was half-naked, still wearing her shoes, excited, but also wary. "Do we need a safe word?"

"'No' works. Do you want me to stop?" His golden-brown eyes glittered with amusement as they met hers.

"You're evil," she accused, since she couldn't answer his question without risking that he would, in fact, stop. "Keep going."

"Tell me what you like." He watched his hand as he trailed his touch down her quivering abdomen to the damp line of her folds. He lightly traced the seam, his touch stirring the fine hairs there until she thought she would die of need.

She bit her lip, breath catching.

"You have to tell me you want this, Evie. Open your legs if you don't want to say it."

She did. And she closed her eyes because it felt so

flagrant to offer herself this way, but he made it worth it. A rumbled noise of approval resounded in his chest as he found her damp with readiness. He opened his mouth over her nipple and sucked while he explored her intimately, stoking the fire that was threatening to consume her. He circled where she pulsed and delved into the ache with one long finger, sliding and caressing while he pulled at her nipple until she thought she would die.

It was too good. She twisted in agonized pleasure, moaning with torture, tense with the struggle of fighting off a climax that had been building since she'd danced with him.

She had never orgasmed with anyone else in the room. Definitely not from someone else delivering it. It made her feel incredibly exposed to let him play with her this way, but the pleasure was so acute, so relentless, she was losing the fight.

He released her nipple. "Do you want my mouth here?" He slowly pressed a second finger into her then eased his touch up to press the swollen, needy, shivering bundle of nerves.

It was the final straw. The coiled tension within her released. She groaned long and loud, catching at his hand to hold it against her mound as she abandoned anything like dignity and bucked, consumed by ecstasy.

His mouth smothered hers, capturing her moans while he caressed her through the crisis and into the shuddering aftermath.

Then he chuckled and freed her arm from beneath her. He shifted over her. His arms caged her beneath him as he settled his still clothed hips against the damp, overly sensitive flesh of her bare pelvis. His hand took hold of her hair in a fist that was just tight enough to keep her head still while he kissed her again, deep and hungry, dragging at her lips and searching out her tongue with his own.

"I'm going to be buried in you to the root when you do that again," he promised when he let her up to breathe.

She couldn't wait. She roamed her hands over his back and into his shorts at his hip, shyly moving her touch forward, but stalling when she heard the muffled xylophone keys of an incoming call on her phone.

"My mother," she muttered in apology. She pulled her hand free of his shorts and searched beneath the bunched blanket where the phone had slid. "I'll turn it off."

As she drew it from the sheets, however, Dom grabbed her wrist. He stared at the screen.

"How the hell do you know that man?" His voice had gone ice-cold.

Jealous? Because it wasn't Ginny Visconti.

"That's Nico. My brother," she said dismissively.

Dom pushed off the bed. Her lover of seconds ago had left the room, the building and the country. *This* was a man who was dangerous.

"You're Evelina Visconti?" His lip curled with repulsion.

"Yes?" She ought to sound more certain. She knew who she was. Kind of. She had never behaved like this with anyone so she was a bit of a stranger to herself in this moment. She was definitely someone else to him, though. Someone he didn't like.

She reached for the edge of the sheet.

"Get the hell out of my hotel."

"Your—What?" She sat up, trying to drag her bra back into place while tucking the blankets across her naked lower half, but he'd already seen everything and was looking at her as though he found her to be the lowest form of filth. "You're not…" He couldn't be. But his name was suddenly drumming in her ears. Dom, Dom, Dom. "You're not Domenico *Blackwood*."

As in Winslow-Blackwood Enterprises? WBE. *No.*

"Don't pretend that's a shock. What the hell is this? Do you have cameras in here or something?" He looked around while pulling his shirt over his head.

"What? No! That's disgusting."

"It is disgusting that you would do something like this. I can't believe how low your family stoops."

"You came onto me," she cried. "You asked to see my room! And my condoms." Along with her breasts and her body and, apparently, her humiliation. She had thought the rivalry between the Blackwoods and Viscontis was ancient history, but it was real and here and she suddenly felt very sick. "Did *you* plan this?"

"No." He looked as outraged at the accusation as she had been. "I would have had you removed if I'd known you were staying here. I'm going to have you removed now."

"Get out of here and I'll remove myself." She hated that crack in her voice. And the scald in her throat that was climbing to press behind her eyes.

"You don't tell me where I go in my own hotel." He punctuated that with a derisive point. Contempt flashed in his bronze gaze as his gaze flickered to the sheet across her waist. "Don't try to use this against me. I'll bury you."

"Same to you," she said in such a puerile response, it only earned her a snort and a final, dismissive curl of his lip.

"Security will be here in twenty minutes. You had better not be." He walked out.

CHAPTER THREE

Six months later...

DOM WALKED INTO his father's empty office and left the lights off, allowing the wet, New York day to cast everything in shades of pewter and ash. It suited his mood.

Not because he was depressed and grieving. His responsibilities were heavy and his thoughts grim, but there was relief in his father's passing. Thomas Blackwood had been a bitter, combative man and, when his heart began to fail, had been even more quick to punish those around him who still possessed optimism for the future.

The funeral had been a somber affair, but there had been a collective exhale from everyone in attendance, Dom's mother especially. Dom's stepmother, Ingrid, had been the only one still projecting tension and discord. She didn't like that she'd lost the ear of the patriarch. She would live out her life in comfort with a suitable allowance, but like everyone else, she was now reliant and beholden to Dom. The heir.

Dom glanced at the open bottle of Scotch in the refreshment nook, but as much as he would like to disappear into oblivion, he had too much to do—starting with fending off the Viscontis.

In the ten days between his father dying in his sleep and his body going into the ground, Romeo Visconti and his three sons had swept across the globe like an invading army.

Granted, WBE wouldn't have been in such a vulnerable position if Thomas Blackwood hadn't insisted on staying at this desk while he had breath in his body. Dom's father had made some terrible decisions in the last years, determined to see the Visconti Group destroyed before he died. Dom had regarded that vendetta as a waste of time, energy, money and resources, but there had been nothing he could do except argue and watch.

Privately, he had hoped the feud between the Blackwoods and Viscontis would end with his father. *He* had been prepared to let it fall away into history since that's all it was.

Dom's great-grandfather had bootlegged and smuggled alcohol with Christopher Winslow during the Great Depression. When Prohibition ended, they turned their stills into breweries and their speakeasies into nightclubs. They invested their ill-gotten gains into hotels and casinos then, to ensure their combined fortunes stayed in the family, they arranged for Maria Winslow to marry Michael Blackwood.

Maria hadn't turned up at the church. She eloped with Aldo Visconti instead.

Humiliated, the Blackwoods did their best to ruin the Winslows, taking ownership of their shared properties and cutting them off from income streams. The Winslows hung onto a few assets, barely, then reconciled with the daughter they had shunned and used Visconti money to rally.

Through the ensuing years, there'd been some territorial disputes between the Blackwoods and the Viscontis, but the fight should have stayed between Michael and Aldo. Dom's grandfather had pushed it into the next generation, though. When his twin sons, Thomas and Peter, had discovered that Romeo Visconti was at Harvard with them, Michael goaded his sons into an academic rivalry with the Visconti heir. That enmity carried into their business dealings when they all began working at their family companies.

A war of empires ensued through the eighties and nineties. Visconti Group and Winslow-Blackwood Enterprises became synonymous with five-star accommodation, luxury entertainments and a battle as competitive as those between the top cola brands. At one point, Romeo had launched a trademark suit, coming at Winslow-Blackwood for continuing to use the Winslow name—which he had no right to, either. The suit itself was frivolous, but he won over public sentiment, forcing the rebranding of Winslow-Blackwood Hotels and Resorts to the less elegant WBE.

Dom had vague memories of his father from those days. Thomas had never been gregarious or fun, but he hadn't been mean. He and his siblings had been the product of a fraught marriage so they were all taciturn people who showed little emotion except anger. Uncle Pete had never married, hadn't had children, but he'd worked side by side with Thomas at WBE. They'd been focused and intent. Workaholics to some extent, because their father constantly whipped them to work harder, be more. *Win*.

After Michael Blackwood died, there'd been another chance to take the personal out of the battle. Elbowing for market share was to be expected, but there was no reason for Dom's father to hold onto a grudge against Romeo.

Perhaps he would have let it go if Romeo hadn't been implicated in Peter's death. Romeo was cleared of wrongdoing, but losing his brother changed Thomas. From then on, he had one goal: to annihilate the Viscontis. His thirst for vengeance cost him his marriage to Dom's mother, but Thomas simply found a wife who agreed with him and kept on his one-track quest to punish.

Dom was sorry for his father's loss. He felt cheated of what might have been a better relationship with him if things had been different. His childhood had been isolating at best and too often punctuated with his father's harsh moods, bullying and unreasonable demands. Dom had shouldered responsibilities well beyond his years, purely because his father was trying to turn him into a foot soldier in his personal war. Dom had been caught in the impossible position of wanting to inherit something he knew inside out, something he believed he could do great things with, but he had to appease the old man to do it.

He had never blamed the Viscontis for any of that. Never hated them or wished them ill.

Until now.

Now those opportunistic carrion-eaters were taking advantage of his father's death to raid and pillage. In a matter of days, they had scooped up majority shares in half a dozen WBE properties that were mid-development. They were buying WBE debts so they could call them. They were attacking Dom on all fronts and *he knew why.*

Evelina.

He dropped into his father's chair, but refused to close his eyes because, whenever he did, all he saw was her. He saw long black hair and long tanned legs. He saw small, high breasts as she twisted in erotic anguish under his touch. He saw white lips shaping his name while her dark brown eyes widened in horror.

For the millionth time, he looked back on every second of his time in Budapest, from his last-minute agreement to oversee the party to how Eve could have made that elevator open at that specific moment. There was no way she could have orchestrated any of it. He was only trying to convince himself that she was a criminal mastermind so he could absolve himself of blame for having touched her.

She hadn't waved him to approach her from across a crowded club. His own feet had carried him there. She hadn't danced with him until he'd asked. She hadn't tried to come home with him.

She hadn't known who he was.

And even though he had relived their interactions a thousand times, punishing himself for not recognizing her, he simply hadn't. Why not? He knew all three of her brothers by sight and reputation, if not personally. He should have seen the resemblance.

Not that she looked much like her older siblings. They had wide jaws and broad shoulders and were full of machismo. Evelina was the happy surprise who was several years younger. Aside from her height, she took after her Italian grandfather's family. That's where she got her black hair and dark brown eyes and that touch of gold embedded in her skin.

She had attended an all-girls boarding school in Switzerland and she'd been too young to be in any of Dom's social circles, not that Visconti and Blackwood worlds were allowed to overlap. After the loss of his brother, Dom's father hadn't allowed a Visconti name to be spoken in his earshot, let alone suffer the presence of one in a room with him. They were "that family" or, if he was referencing Romeo, "the mongrel."

Thus, Dom hadn't had a clue he was lusting after Romeo's daughter that night.

All he'd known when the elevator opened was that he couldn't let her go again. Compelled by what could only be called a primitive imperative, Dom had made all the advances, barely capable of his usual restraint. He always made sure a woman wanted his sexual attention, but he'd been more assertive than usual. More driven.

Eve had seemed surprised by his directness, but when it came down to it, she'd matched his level of carnality. That's what still made him hard in a heartbeat, that she'd trembled and moaned and climaxed when he'd barely touched her.

He'd wanted inside her more than he'd wanted his next breath.

At that point, the gods had had their biggest laugh at his expense. They'd delivered the message he'd so far failed to grasp. Her phone rang and there was Nico Visconti's smug face turning Dom's lust to disgust. To ire at being thwarted. And rage at feeling tricked.

Eve had seemed equally aghast. Maybe it really had been a series of outlandish coincidences, but their innocent mistake didn't make any of their actions less criminal. Not in his mind. Certainly not in the mind of his father if he ever found out.

For weeks, Dom had debated coming clean about the incident, wanting to get ahead of his father's tantrum. No matter how or when Thomas learned of the betrayal, it could literally stop his heart.

Ultimately, Dom had stayed silent not out of shame or concern for his father, but from a misguided sense of decency. He had sisters. He knew that pinning a Scarlet A on a woman, humiliating her for having a sexual appetite, was as sexist and hypocritical as it got. His father would do it anyway. If it would hurt Romeo to have his daughter disgraced, Thomas would revel in making her suffer.

Dom's heart was not quite as charred as his father's. He kept his mouth shut and waited to see if she would move first. If *she* would reveal the intimate things they'd done.

There'd been nothing but silence.

Until his father died.

Now Eve's father and brothers were jumping on WBE

like hyenas on a wounded gazelle. There was a small chance they were acting independently, Dom supposed. As far as he could tell, Eve had recently been given a midlevel position with their head office so she didn't have the frontline ability to lead these sorts of attacks, but she easily could have spun some story to her father that would fuel this action.

Either way, Dom's father was dead. That meant the Viscontis were coming for *him*.

Dom understood his father's perspective now, even his grandfather's. The Viscontis were leaving him with no choice but to fight. He was angry enough at their tactics that he wouldn't rest until he had his teeth in their proverbial throats.

A memory flashed of the mark he'd left on Eve's neck. Heat pooled behind his fly.

Damn it, he wanted her out of his head! He wanted her and her family relegated to the fringes of his perception, where he would never think about any of them ever again.

It might take years. It might take playing the wounded antelope to lead them down a path toward an ambush, but he was a smart, patient man. He could do it.

One way or another, he would end this feud once and for all.

CHAPTER FOUR

Four years later...

HE WAS HERE. God help her, Dom Blackwood was attending this freaking wedding.

Which wouldn't be such a nightmare if it had been a typical afternoon-evening affair, but no. This was a weeklong extravaganza in the Whitsunday Islands of Australia.

How many times had she considered calling off her agreement to come? Every day since she'd been asked. Eve didn't even know the couple getting married. She was the plus-one for a man she'd only been seeing for two months.

Her date, Logan Offerman, was a handsome lawyer with political aspirations who came from a big family with old money. He liked dogs and hiking and supported right-to-vote legislation. He had gone to school with her middle brother, Jackson. His parents were friends of her own from the country club.

Eve's mother, who had always told Eve to guard her virginity like it was the Hope diamond, wanted this marriage. Everyone did. Her father kept saying, "It's a good match." Her eldest brother, Nico, was starting to sound like a used car salesman, he was selling it so hard. Her youngest brother, Christopher, was indifferent, but happy that she was taking the heat of family attention so he could live his bohemian life in Hawaii unbothered.

Ginny had essentially poked a sword in Eve's back to get her onto the plane.

"Spend some time with him. You'll soon see how right this is for both of you." Eve suspected her mother believed that if Eve finally slept with a man, she might actually marry him.

Eve had been finding fault with her mother's suggested suitors for four years. Even she was tired of it. She really, really wanted to fall for Logan, if only to finally have some peace from this constant pressure to marry. Nevertheless, all she could think was that Logan reminded her of sunscreen. He offered important protection, but made her feel sticky and suffocated.

Logan was a groomsman in the wedding party so they'd been given a beautiful two-bedroom suite at the eco-resort where the guests without yachts were being housed. Eve knew that Logan was hoping they would start sleeping together while they were away. He didn't take it for granted, though. He set her suitcase in the second bedroom without asking, only sending her a brief, hopeful look that resembled a puppy tapping its tail.

"I think I'll nap before the welcome reception," Eve said, closing herself into her room.

She was actually going to scream into her pillow because what else could she do?

While they'd been ferried across from the mainland

with some of the other wedding guests, she'd overheard someone ask a very beautiful woman, "Isn't Dom with you?"

"WBE just bought a hotel in Airlie Beach," the woman had replied. "He's staying there for meetings. I want time with my family and I'm a bridesmaid so…"

Eve had drifted away, ostensibly to enjoy the view, but mostly because she had feared she would lose her breakfast over the rail.

She had managed to avoid Domenico Blackwood for four years—mostly. She had compulsively learned far too much about him online from how many women he dated to the fact he was named for his mother's favorite uncle. He lived in New York, but he had properties around the world and was very hands-on so he was rarely home.

Even when he was there, the chance of running into him was low. Her parents were very good about vetting guest lists. There had only been a handful of times that Eve had glimpsed Dom from across a restaurant. The one time she had walked into a Fourth of July party and noticed him, she had claimed a migraine and left immediately.

Each tiny encounter had left her unable to sleep for days, though, always wondering if he'd seen her and whether he would finally turn on her, exposing her behavior to her family and anyone else who would listen. Over the years, she had only grown more mortified by the way she had behaved with him in Budapest. The fact he'd been a stranger was embarrassing enough, but her father had genuinely hated Dom's.

Romeo's hostility toward Thomas Blackwood was understandable. The man had accused him of murder, but it had all been cleared up. Nevertheless, when Thomas had died, her father had rallied her brothers to attack WBE.

Eve had questioned her father on that. It seemed like a dirty move when Dom had been grieving and finding his feet as the head of the company.

"Michael Blackwood didn't let up on me when *my* father died," her father groused.

At that point, Eve had distanced herself, still unable to think of how uninhibited she'd been without cringing. Dom had both ignited and derailed her passion, making it impossible for her to feel anything with anyone else.

Eventually, her father had determined WBE was on its last legs. He had retired and handed the reins to Nico.

Eve should have seen an upward trajectory in her own career at that point, but Dom and WBE had quickly begun to rally, apparently not so beaten as they'd seemed. Nico spent all his time countering offensives while she was left to languish in the marketing division. In fact, the resort that Dom had just purchased here in Queensland had been targeted as the next Visconti property. Nico was furious that he had not only lost to Dom *again*, but had lost the significant time and money he'd put into his attempt to acquire it.

Eve couldn't help wondering if Dom's relentless attack was fueled by what had happened between them. She hadn't told a soul about meeting him in Budapest and never would, but dreaded that Dom might. He could be waiting for exactly the right moment to slay her with a pithy revelation that would destroy her reputation, turn her family into a mockery and lower her family's view of her.

She hated that he held that over her!

Her stomach churned as she dressed for the welcome reception two hours later. The schedule of mix-and-mingle activities through the week included day trips and shopping, sailing and diving and hiking, all culminating in the ceremony and reception five days from now. It was organized like an all-inclusive trade conference, which was the real reason she had accepted this invitation. Her middle brother, Jackson, had reminded her that there would be a lot of quality connections to be made.

"Bring value to the table," he had advised her, well aware of how frustrated she was with their older brother's reluctance to advance her in the company. "That's the kind of thing Nico notices and appreciates."

Nico did nothing but stonewall her. No matter how hard she worked, he treated her as though she was five, not twenty-five, but Eve was willing to try anything to get him to take her seriously.

Even face Dom again.

Or maybe not. Ugh. She was regretting everything about being here as she and Logan arrived at the outdoor dining room—including the fact that she'd left her hair down because there was just enough breeze and humidity to make tiny strands stick to her face and neck.

Running back to her suite for a scarf wasn't an option. It would look like another retreat, not that Dom even noticed her, but *she* would know that she was being a coward.

After her first sweeping glance—and the painful

awareness that sliced through her when she spotted him—she looked anywhere but where he stood with the tall brunette she'd overheard earlier. Was that woman his wife? His fiancée? He'd been engaged ages ago, before they'd met, but nothing of the sort had been reported lately.

Not that she cared.

Eve barely noticed what the other woman looked like. Dom's image dominated her vision. She forced herself to smile as they began moving through the receiving line, but all she saw was Dom's athletic frame in bone-colored trousers and a pale blue Henley in fine cotton. His jaw was shaved clean which made him look even tougher than when he'd worn stubble. Maybe it was the aviator glasses reflecting the sinking sun against the water that gave him such an air of remote arrogance. Maybe it was a stronger air of command that had developed in response to his takeover at WBE.

Maybe it was the same belly-deep loathing for an adversary that sat in her own stomach.

But who is your loathing really for? a sneering voice mocked deep inside her.

It was for herself. She had been so *eager* that morning in Budapest. So *easy.* It was the great irony of her life that she'd resorted to telling men she was waiting for marriage as an excuse for not sleeping with them. The truth was, the only man she'd ever wanted to have sex with was that man, the one she hated most on earth. The very last man she would ever touch.

Logan introduced her to the bride and groom and their parents.

Eve forced her bright smile to stay in place as the mother of the bride drew her aside. "I'm so sorry, dear. I was just informed of the bad blood between you and one of our guests."

"What?" A wet sack of cement landed in her gut.

"The professional rivalry between the Viscontis and the Blackwoods. Dom is here as a guest of my niece." The woman glanced over, but Eve refused to give in to the temptation to do the same. "I wouldn't want anyone to be uncomfortable..." The woman meant her niece and her daughter, the bride.

"Are you referring to the court case between our fathers?" Eve asked with manufactured confusion. "Oh, that trademark dispute was settled ages ago. It's old news." She dismissed it with a wave of her hand. "Besides, I understand there are more than seventy islands to explore here. I doubt we'll even speak." She leaned in to add with forced levity, "Maybe don't seat us together, just to be sure."

The woman chuckled with relief and went back to the receiving line.

Eve took a subtle, shaken breath, hoping her request would be taken seriously. She absolutely did not want to talk to Dom.

"Everything all right?" Logan appeared beside her to offer a glass of white wine.

"Mmm. She...um...warned me that Dom Blackwood is here. I've never met him." She used the excuse to glance around, deliberately looking the wrong direction.

"Over my left shoulder. Your brother won't be happy," Logan said ruefully.

Eve did her best to appear disinterested, sipping and glancing past Logan.

Dom's attention seemed angled her way, but with his mirrored sunglasses it was impossible to tell if he was looking at her. Her heart rattled in her chest anyway. Hot coals of yearning glowed brighter in her midsection. It was shameful to react this way. It took all of her control to hide her response behind a blank expression.

You mean nothing to me, she transmitted, before looking to Logan with a sweet smile.

"What do you want to do tomorrow?"

She really did hate Dom, she decided, as Logan's voice turned into a drone that was as pesky as a mosquito's whine while the rest of her senses were amplified with proprioception.

Dom had broken her with their early-morning dalliance in Budapest. No one had ever made her feel so much want. For the first time, she had let herself go with what she was feeling. She had let him see her at her most vulnerable, in the throes of passion. She had been in a state of shock, half-naked, the rest of her clothing askew, when he had ordered her to leave.

She had felt rejected and dirty and mortified as she hurried to pack. She hadn't wanted to stay another second. She had texted Hailey on her way to the airport that something had come up and she'd waited with trepidation for Dom to say something to the press or leak something on a grapevine. She had been sure he would use her behavior against her.

He hadn't. Which was no consolation. She only felt beneath his notice, which was somehow worse. He seemed to have wiped her from his mind and she ought to be able to do the same. It was her deepest shame that she still fantasized about him.

Did he touch that woman's arm? A barb of envy pierced her chest. Now her ears strained for his voice, hearing him order a drink with, "Extra ice."

"What do you think?" Logan asked.

She bit back a bewildered, *What?* He'd been saying something about snorkeling off the groom's yacht, but she hadn't been paying attention.

"That sounds fun." She kept her smile on her face even though Dom moved closer, to speak to a couple nearby.

Her back felt his presence like a tropical sun was radiating a third-degree burn into her skin.

Logan, bless him, said, "Darling, come meet my friend Dave and his wife."

The whole evening was like that, drifting into striking distance of a deadly viper, trying not to draw Dom's attention while gripped by tension, waiting for him to say something to her or about her or force her to speak to him.

Most disgraceful of all, when she and Logan were on their way to her room, all she could wonder was whether that cousin of the bride would be screaming Dom's name later.

"He's staying at his property on the mainland," Logan said as the door to their suite closed behind them.

"Pardon?" Good God. She hadn't spoken her thoughts aloud, had she?

"Blackwood. I checked. And I texted your brother,

letting him know I'll make sure he doesn't bother you, so you can relax."

Eve blinked, wondering if she was supposed to be flattered that Logan was acting so proprietary, as though she couldn't make her own decisions or look after herself.

"I would have thought all of that rivalry had died with his father," Logan continued as he casually kicked off his shoes and left them in the middle of the floor. "Your brother sounded pretty agitated, though, asking whether WBE was expanding elsewhere in Australia, beyond that resort he just bought. I said I'd ask around."

"Boys will be boys," Eve said blithely. "I don't pay much attention."

That was another huge lie. She wished she could ignore Dom and what her brother did to antagonize him, but she couldn't. She should probably be grateful she was still being held at arm's length from the top-level decisions or she might betray her excess interest, but she was mostly indignant at being relegated to branding and décor, never included in big decisions or given real responsibilities.

A light hand slid along her arm. She tensed in something that felt a lot like repulsion.

"Darling? I respect that you want to wait until your wedding night, but... We could do other things," Logan persuaded. "Perhaps get in the hot tub and see what happens?" He nodded toward the terrace.

"I have a headache." Not a lie. "Can we talk about that tomorrow?"

"Of course. But if you're going to bed, I'll change and

pop down for a nightcap." At least he didn't pout about it. Maybe marriage to him would be okay.

"Sleep well." He kissed her cheek, leaving her cold.

"Of all the gin joints in all the towns..."

Dom had thought those grim words more times than Bogart himself had said them. Why that night, in that bar, in that rabbit warren of a playground in Budapest? Why *her*? A Visconti?

And why was he still fascinated by her four years after he had resolved to erase her from his mind?

Because he still carried a sense of something unfinished. It was no mystery why. He hadn't slept with anyone since. No matter how sexually frustrated he got, no matter how beautiful and receptive his date might be, they all left him unmoved.

Yet all Eve Visconti had to do was lift her hair off the back of her neck and he was hard as a rock, barely able to restrain himself.

Aside from one haughty glance past her lover's ear, she had avoided looking at him during the welcome reception last night. Yes, he had noticed, even though he'd done his best to ignore her, too. It was a skill he'd perfected the handful of times he'd seen her in New York. It didn't matter if he looked at her or not, though. His inner radar always tracked her when she was in the vicinity. He knew where she was and which man she spoke to and how she sounded when she climaxed.

When she'd left the party last night, Dom's blood had turned to acid as he wondered whether that stick puppet of an attorney was making her shatter. He hadn't slept and blamed her for that, too.

Now he'd arrived for a buffet brunch and beach activities. He was pretending not to notice Eve as she came out of the pool. Her wide-brimmed hat and retro sunglasses hid most of her face, but her lithe figure was on full display in a red one-piece with waist cutouts. Her nipples hardened despite the full sun of midmorning. Water beaded against her golden skin. Her legs were still a mile and a half each way, accentuated by the high cut of her suit and the heeled sandals she stepped into. She accepted a towel from that toothpaste ad of a boyfriend.

"—need a special permit because they limit access. If we want to see it, we have to go tomorrow."

Dom dragged his gaze off the pert cheeks of Evie's ass where the V of her suit left a portion of the pale globes bare and looked to the pretty face tilted up to his.

"They're expecting a storm, though," Cat continued. "We have to be off the island by two. My brother will take us on his sailboat."

"Okay." Dom wished he'd brought his own yacht or at least rented one. He had a speedboat operator at his beck and call, but anything larger had seemed superfluous when he had the penthouse in his new, five-star hotel on the mainland—the one he'd scooped away from Eve's brother.

Dom's battle with Nico for key properties was coming out in his favor almost exclusively these days. When he'd taken over WBE, it had been struggling, but he'd shored up its cash position and had a sizable cushion these days, one that allowed him to enter bidding wars that forced Visconti Group to either back off or pay through the nose for what they wanted.

Dom had a strong feeling that financial pressure was the reason Eve was here with Logan Offerman, second son of a multimedia tycoon.

"The kids will be aboard," Cat added with an appealing expression.

Dom made himself pay attention to what she was saying. Spending time with Cat and her family was the point of his being here. His middle sister had set him up with Cat, urging him to be her date to this wedding since he was planning a trip to Australia anyway.

Dom was trying, genuinely trying, to like her. Cat was everything he ought to look for in a life partner—well-mannered, well-connected and well-off. Children liked her. So did his sister and, seemingly, everyone else.

"Oh!"

The startled pitch in Eve's voice snapped Dom's head around while his muscles bunched in readiness to attack.

She wasn't being assaulted, though. Her hat had blown off. It rolled toward him and fetched up against his feet.

She chased it with long strides of those forever legs and halted when he straightened to offer it to her.

They both wore sunglasses, but he knew they looked straight into each other's eyes. He felt the clash all the way into his chest. Lower.

She had shrugged on a cover-up of eyelet lace. Belting it had probably been the reason she'd failed to catch her hat.

"Thank you." She swallowed as she took it, then

pressed something that looked like a natural smile onto her face as she said to Cat, "I apologize for interrupting."

"No problem. I'm Catherine. Cat." She offered her hand. "Have you met Dom?"

"I haven't. Eve. Nice to meet you both." She briefly shook Cat's hand, aimed a polite smile vaguely but not quite in his direction and said, "I won't keep you. Excuse me."

Dom bit back a hoot of laughter. They hadn't met? *Wow.*

Eve set her hat on her head and walked away with long, unhurried strides that made his blood itch.

"The animosity is real," Cat said in an undertone of amusement. "She didn't even shake your hand."

He had noticed. His palm felt scorched yet empty.

"Shall we get out on the Jet Skis before they're gone?" Dom suggested. He was too much of a workaholic to get much pleasure from such a pointless activity, but the greater goal was to get to know Cat. He was testing the waters, so to speak, considering whether to pursue a more formal arrangement.

He followed Cat toward the rental shack on the wharf, fighting the urge to look back at Eve.

He lost.

CHAPTER FIVE

EVE HAD TO hand it to Logan. He'd taught her to carry a sensible assortment of items when leaving for a day hike—most of which turned out to be unnecessary today. They arrived with the rest of the guests at one of the uninhabited islands to find the groom's family had installed a pop-up store and takeaway shack on the beach.

The shack was on pontoons so it could be floated back to whence it had come, once the day was over. Its large wooden awning was levered up with poles to shade the order window. Racks of sarongs, beach towels, flip-flops and sunhats stood nearby.

"This was arranged last year, before they knew there'd be a storm," Eve overheard someone say while she was flicking through the sarongs. "They thought everyone would be swimming and snorkeling all day then dancing on the beach until sunrise. The band will perform at the resort tonight instead."

At least there was a portable loo. Eve used it before heading out with Logan across the island.

Logan was hungover after the stag party on the mainland last night. There'd been a hen party for the bride at the resort, but Eve had been happy to stay alone in the suite, catching up on reading after she composed a blistering email to her brother asking him to read her most recent proposal and give her the promotion she deserved.

She was taking out her frustration with Dom's imposing presence on her brother, sure, but she wasn't wrong.

Whether Dom had joined the stag party, she didn't know. He had looked fresh as a daisy when he had waded in from one of the other boats. He wore loose swim shorts in shades of blue with a white surf shirt that hugged his torso so lovingly, she could count the muscles in his six-pack.

Disgusted with herself for noticing, Eve set a grumpy pace along the trail to the far side of the island. The track climbed up through the rainforest then across the top of a hill that opened into grassland. When they arrived at a lookout, they paused to photograph the stunning views of empty islands surrounded by swirls of white sand and turquoise waters.

The track then descended toward a bottle tree and a sign that marked a split in the track. One read Spit, the other Turtle Bay.

They chose turtles and descended to a private beach of powder-white sand with a sea turtle sunning itself in the lapping surf.

"This is beautiful." Eve stayed well back from the creature, but used the zoom feature on her phone to snap a photo of it.

"I think I'm going to be sick." Logan braced his hands on his knees. His face glowed with perspiration. "This isn't normal behavior for me," he assured her as he looked to the scrub at the edge of the beach. "Just old friends behaving like we're still in college. Oh, I meant to ask you…" Logan straightened to take out his electrolyte drink and sip it. "I picked up a text from your brother before we left. He asked me if Dom is upsetting you. Is he?"

"What? No. Why would he?" She lowered her phone, growing prickly. *From the heat.*

"I don't know." Logan shrugged. "Nico said you sent him an email that sounded bitchy. His word." He held up a staying hand as she snapped her spine straight.

"That doesn't make it okay to repeat! And wouldn't you be bitchy if you were being held back every second of every day?"

"He's not holding you back." He took another pull off his drink. "He's being realistic."

"In what way?" Why was he taking her brother's side?

"I'm not trying to insult you, Eve." His tone said, *calm down.*

"Yet you're managing to." She strained to sound ultra-reasonable instead of incredibly irritated, which she was. "I think it's very realistic that, after four years of dedicated service, my brother give me more responsibility in the family company. When Jackson was twenty-five, he was given all of Europe to oversee. Christo has the Pacific Rim. I'm not even *head* of marketing yet."

"Because Nico knows that you *claim* you want a top position in the business, but that will change once you're married and have children."

"I'm not *claiming* to want it. I know what I want." And she was affronted that Logan seemed to doubt that.

"A husband and children could be years away. I don't know how I'll feel when that happens so how could Nico?"

"Years?" Logan's brows crinkled with a patronizing aren't-you-cute? expression. "Darling, we have to marry within the year so I can hit the ground running with the next campaign cycle. If you want to put off children for a short time after that, I suppose I can agree, but voters prefer family men, not power wives who put their career ahead of their husband's. I think you'll find that between raising our children and keeping up with the duties of a congressman's wife, you won't have time to spare for Visconti Group. Which is what I told your brother when you and I started dating—"

"Oh, my God," she cut in, putting up a staying hand. "Was that your marriage proposal to me just now? I respectfully decline."

"Eve." His mouth tightened with dismay. "Don't be like that."

"I'm not saying that with hard feelings, Logan. Honestly. I'm glad we've established that we want different things." In fact, she was profoundly relieved. "I'll go back to the landing beach where I will catch a lift with the first boat willing to take me to the hotel. Then I'll pack and leave you to enjoy the wedding and the rest of your life with whoever wants to dedicate her life to being your wife and only your wife, because that woman isn't me."

"Wait, stop. Come on. You can't leave. What would I tell people?" He put out a pleading hand.

"Say I had a family emergency." She paused in starting toward the track. "My brother will definitely need surgery to remove the job I'm about to shove up his—"

Logan cursed and clutched his stomach, then staggered toward the weeds.

What a catch.

"Bye, Logan." She spun to push herself up the winding incline with such force, her thigh muscles burned. She was impelled by anger at Logan and his assumptions, and her brother and his sexist dismissal of her, and her whole family for only seeing she had value as a wife, not as an employee. Not as a person.

She was panting and sweating as she arrived at the bottle tree in time to hear Dom and Cat on the lookout above her, taking photos.

Ugh. He was the *last* person she wanted to see when she was ready to burn down the patriarchy with the sheer force of her glare.

She veered down the track labeled Spit. It had taken less than an hour to hike across the island and the boats weren't leaving until two. She would easily get back in time.

Or so she believed.

Dom was not a quitter, but nor was he a liar.

This wasn't working with Cat. She leaned into him, eyes limpid, mouth soft and inviting and all he could think was, *Don't.*

He couldn't reject her days before she was supposed to be a bridesmaid in her cousin's wedding, though.

At least they weren't sleeping together. She might accuse him of leading her on when they had The Talk, but he'd barely kissed her cheek since a certain someone had arrived under his nose to torture him all over again.

"Dom?" Cat murmured, drawing a circle around the small logo above his heart. "Are we o—? Oh!" With a self-conscious smile, she stepped away, glancing beyond him. "Hi."

Dom turned to see Logan coming up from the trail down to the far side of the island. He was sweaty and red-faced with exertion. He paused to give them a curt nod of greeting.

Dom braced himself for the sight of Eve, but she didn't appear behind him.

"Where's Eve?" Cat asked, looking past him.

"She had to leave," Logan said with a sullen pout. "Family emergency."

When? Dom had seen her leaving on her walk with Logan and they would have passed her on the trail if she'd already gone back. Or Dom would have felt her walk behind him while they were taking photos. He didn't *want* a sixth sense where she was concerned, but he had one.

"Is it worth hiking down to see the turtles?" Cat asked Logan.

"There was only one and it went back into the water. I'll see you at the thing later." Logan's gaze refused to meet his, striking Dom as shifty before Logan headed back to the cove where the boats were mustered.

Dom didn't think the other man had done anything nefarious to Eve, but a sense of wrongness abraded his insides as the other man left. Dom's ears felt pricked for her voice, his nose twitching to catch her scent.

"Trouble in paradise?" Cat elevated her brows in amused speculation.

Dom shrugged, irritated by the question. "Do you want to see the turtles?"

"He said there weren't any. If it's just a beach, let's go back to the one we can swim at."

The weather was turning cloudy and the water was too choppy for comfortable snorkeling. That's why they had decided to walk instead of swim. Dom was reluctant to leave the trail, though. It was a gut-level response that he relied on when he made big decisions at WBE, the kind that wasn't always backed up by logic and facts, but never steered him wrong.

Leaving the trail went against his instinct, but he took Cat back to the cove, compelled to see if Eve was, in fact, there.

She was officially an unhealthy obsession, he decided, when they arrived and he couldn't see her. He scanned the crowd and counted the boats, noting that one yacht had left. It was feasible she'd been taken back to the resort. She wasn't his responsibility anyway. She was his *enemy*, for God's sake. Her whole family was a pile of thorns in his side.

He told Cat to swim without him and pondered whether to radio a boat he couldn't identify while he watched Logan pour margaritas down his throat as though he was being paid to do it. Guilty conscience? *Was* there trouble in paradise?

"She had to leave," he overheard Logan say to someone. "Family emergency."

Dom knew he was behaving like a Victorian spinster, worrying about someone he had no business caring about, but he couldn't shake a sense that Eve was still here. Just not *here*.

As the wind picked up and the first raindrops fell, boats began pulling in gear and families started gathering children and toys from the beach. Two boats left and the one that had been missing came back from circumnavigating the island. Eve wasn't on it.

"Go with your brother. I'll find someone going to the mainland," Dom said to Cat, glancing at his watch. "I'll catch up to you at dinner."

Cat was surprised, but her sister-in-law asked for her help getting the children to the sailboat so she moved down the beach.

Dom glanced at the takeaway shack, thinking to tell the man running it not to leave until he'd checked back in with him, but Cat's uncle was at the window.

Dom veered from admitting aloud that he was concerned about Eve. He barely wanted to admit it to himself. She was likely fine and had done exactly as Logan had said. She'd made her way back to the eco-resort and was on her way to the airport.

He glanced at his watch again, deciding to be sure. He worked out constantly, both cardio and strength. He could easily sprint across the island and be back before this regatta of disorganized boaters had launched itself.

He slipped into the trees and ran up the track, seizing the challenge, grateful for the sting of rain as he traversed the plateau, keeping him from overheating.

The goat track down to Turtle Beach tested his agility and the area was reassuringly empty. Logan hadn't murdered her.

Dom decided to seek counselling when he got back to New York. This fixation he had developed wasn't healthy.

He started climbing back up and almost ignored the sign labeled Spit, but his feet took him that direction before he'd consciously recollected Logan's assertion that Eve had gone ahead.

A strange tingle hit him as he began jogging that direction. It was the same subconscious polarity that oriented him in an unfamiliar city back to his hotel or car. The same tingle that said, *She's here.*

Just as he began to think he'd been bitten by a hallucinogenic spider, he heard a feminine voice swear a blistering and imaginative blue streak.

Relief crashed over him like a surge of surf, followed by a disorienting anger. Could she not tell time? Now they would arrive back at the resort together and have to make stupid explanations—

He came around a bend in the path and saw she was hurt. She was using a stick of driftwood as a cane. Her foot was out of her shoe with only her toes tucked into it as she limped-slid it forward. She was watching where she put her feet against the various roots protruding across the path, continuing to spill robust curses.

Her ankle was the size of a grapefruit and grossly discolored.

His heart stopped.

"Did something bite you?" That was bad. In this country, that could be very, very bad.

She snapped her head up. Her expression blanked before she cried indignantly to the sky, "Really? *This* is the help you send me?"

"Eve," he said through his teeth. "Did something sting or bite you?"

"*No.* I turned my ankle. It's sprained."

He looked again and realized the bulge was actually an ice pack secured with—

"Is that a *condom*?"

"News flash, they can be used for other things. I took an ibuprofen, but I can't walk on this foot. Can you go tell the boats to wait?"

"I'm sure they'll do a head count." He was not sure of that at all, or of its accuracy, given how people had been jumping on and off each other's boats. "The kid in the takeaway shack won't leave until everyone else does." He hoped.

Dom moved to her side and slipped his arm around her. They both jolted at the electrical charge that zapped like an entire winter's worth of static between them.

She glared at him. He glared back.

She shrugged him off and tried to continue walking without holding onto him.

"Don't be stupid, Eve. You can't do this without—"

"Don't call me stupid." She squared to face him, chin set at a belligerent angle.

Screw it. They could stand here and fight, missing the last boat, or he could duck, which he did, and throw her over his shoulder, which he also did.

"Don't you dare!" she screamed as he straightened

from grabbing her shoe. The day pack she wore slumped to knock into the top of his ass.

"Give me that." He reached back to tug it free of her flailing arms and looped it over his free shoulder so the sack was against his chest.

"Put me down you freaking *animal*." She kicked her feet and braced a hand against his spine, trying to straighten.

"Watch your head," he commanded as he started back the way he'd come.

"Put me *down*." She slapped his ass hard enough to sting.

"Bad news, Evie. I *like* that." He did. Not because he had a kinky streak—although he did have a small one—but more because finally, finally, he was discharging some of his pent-up sexual energy. He wanted a tussle and a pillow fight and *sex*. Raw, dirty, endless sex.

He would settle for a slap on his ass and her weight on his shoulder while he puffed his way up the hill, muscles seared with strain. Her filthy mouth calling him filthy names while her hands clutched into his shirt and her breasts brushed his back was a dream come true.

She tried grabbing the sign as they passed the bottle tree.

"Settle down." He gave her butt a warning tap, very tempted to let his hand linger there. "No one knows I came looking for you. We have to hurry or we'll be stuck here."

"I would rather fall down a crevasse and be eaten by goannas than be held by you."

"You think I woke up today hoping I could run a marathon with radioactive waste on my shoulder?" They arrived at where the lookout gave a view of the back side of the island. He turned a slow circle. "See any boats?"

"No," she said on a whimper.

"Hold onto my waist so you don't bounce. I have to hurry."

With another infuriated noise, she sagged down and hugged her arms around his chest. The temperature was dropping. Clouds were thickening on the horizon and fat, spattering rain was starting to soak their clothes.

"Why are you even here?" she mumbled into his back.

"Why are you?"

She didn't answer, but after a few minutes of his half jog across the grassland stretch, she said, "This hurts my stomach."

"I just want to get to..." He swore as he arrived at the spot where they could see the stretch of water toward the main island. He let her slide down and braced her while she balanced on one foot.

She lifted her hand to shield her eyes from the rain and followed his gaze to the loose armada of boats already well into the distance.

"That little silver one at the back is the kid from the shack." At least he wasn't towing the shed, probably because the water was too rough.

A desolate noise broke from her throat. "They'll do a head count when they get back, though, won't they?"

"Some of them are going to the mainland. Cat thinks I caught one of those. I won't be missed until dinner." He looked to the desperation on her face. "Logan said you had a family emergency?"

"Don't get excited. Everyone's fine," she said crossly. "I told him to say that to cover the fact I was leaving early." She chewed her lip. "Hopefully, he'll notice my things are still in my room and wonder where I am."

"*Your* room? You two aren't sleeping together?" Satisfaction shouldn't have glowed so ember-hot in the pit of his gut at that news. "Is that why you were fighting?"

She scowled resentfully. "What makes you think we were fighting?"

"You're making up reasons to leave early. He was doing his best to get drunk once he got back to the beach. He won't notice you're missing." He shook his head.

"Men are the bane of my existence," she muttered, fists in knots beside her hips.

"So you don't need a lift the rest of the way to the beach?" he asked with false pleasantness.

"Why are you even helping me?" Her voice strained with aggravated emotion.

"Because I don't have your father's stark absence of conscience when it comes to leaving people to die."

CHAPTER SIX

"THAT WAS A cheap shot." Eve was both hot and cold. Her blood was simmering with a mix of anxiety and sexual frustration. Rain was beginning in earnest, soaking her clothes enough to chill her skin as the wind cut across the top of the island. Her ankle hurt. A lot.

She resented the hell out of this man whom she had tried to avoid by taking that stupid trail and wound up injured and stranded and alone. Now she was stuck with him and he thought he could throw old lies in her face?

"I will make my own way down thanks." She would crawl if she had to.

He swore under his breath and ducked again, moving so fast he had her over his shoulder before she could finish her cry of protest.

She didn't bother struggling, though. She passionately hated relying on him, but this was a more efficient way of traveling, especially down the knotty, zigzag path through the rainforest.

Plus, there was a part of her that thrived on the feel of his strong body shifting and flexing under hers. She reveled in the excuse to pin her arms around his chest, hugging herself into his strength while pressing her face into the smell of his skin beneath his shirt.

They didn't speak until they were on the beach. Which was empty. Very, very empty.

She pulled open the Velcro pocket of her shorts and took out her phone. There was no signal here, either. The entire island was out of range.

With a huff of despair, she limped her way into the loo, thankful for *that* small mercy.

When she came out waving her hands, drying the disinfecting lotion, Dom was at the door of the shack, scowling at the locked knob.

"Got a hairpin? I can't kick it in. It opens out."

"What about the window?" The wooden awning was secured with two dead bolts on either side, neither of which was locked.

She slipped each free and Dom lifted the awning, propping it with the dangling sticks. The sliding order window was small, but it slid open when she reached up to touch it.

"Look at us with our teamwork," she said with a sunny smile of triumph.

It faded as she glimpsed his humorless expression.

He linked his hands and bent to offer a stirrup. "Knee," he said. "See if you can unlock the door from the inside."

Oh, this was going to be even more graceful than being slung over his shoulder.

She took hold of the window ledge and set the knee of her injured foot into his hands.

In another show of his supreme strength, he boosted

her high enough she dove headfirst through the opening where she knocked a few caddies of condiments and utensils to the floor.

She caught at the counter on the far side as she dragged her feet in, then under, herself. There wasn't much room to step, though.

"Good news. We can get roaring drunk," she told him through the window as she picked her way over crates of alcohol and around the racks of sarongs and towels to reach out and flick the lock.

He opened the door from the outside and peered in. "Radio?"

She looked around. "No."

Another curse, one with more resignation than heat.

"He has to come back for it at some point," she said.

Dom made a noise of agreement and took the well-used plastic milk crate from inside the door. He set it as a step, then reached for the nearest box of bottles. "I'll throw some of this underneath so we can both fit in there."

There was only a small strip of floor between the counters and the cupboards that lined the walls. The back of the shack held a sink, a stove and a deep fryer that was covered and thankfully empty, despite the lingering funk of grease. The front counter serviced the window. Beneath it was a small refrigerator stocked with bottled water and a few unopened jars of pickles, but little else. The cupboards over the window held canned and dry goods. The ones at the back were full of cooking implements.

Eve stowed what she could of the things she'd

knocked over and stacked the sarongs and beach towels onto the shelf by the window, since they would only blow away or fill with sand if they were left outside.

When the last rack and box of alcohol was removed, she hitched to sit on the counter beside the sink, instantly feeling claustrophobic when Dom stepped inside.

He set a six-pack of premade Bloody Mary cocktails on the ledge by the window.

"It looked like the only thing with nutritional value." His shirt and hair were soaked. His nipples were sharp points beneath his shirt.

Not that she noticed.

She handed him a towel. He ran it over his face and hair, then his bare arms.

He'd secured the door open, but it rattled in the growing wind as did the awning. She made herself look at those things, then above where the rain had become a steady drum on the roof.

"Power?" he asked, flicking a switch by the door.

Nothing happened.

"He must have taken the generator with him." He released another tired curse and gave his damp face a final swipe before tossing the towel onto the pile of clean ones. "Why the hell didn't you come straight back to the beach when you left Logan?"

"Really?" Just like that, her temper was back at explosive. "You want to make this *my* fault? I didn't want to see you," she spelled out belligerently. "Okay? You were standing at the lookout with your girlfriend and I was sick of men, given what Logan had done—"

"What did Logan do?" he asked in a tone that was so lethal, her scalp prickled.

"He said something to my brother that I didn't like," she grumbled. "Why didn't you tell someone you thought I was missing and ask them to find me?"

He muttered something about this being an unproductive conversation and closed both window and door, leaving the awning open to provide light and a view of the heavy surf as it crashed onto shore.

"Is there anything to eat?" He started to open a cupboard.

"Potato chips and candy bars, crackers and caviar, pickles and olives, canned pineapple and beets. When that runs out, each other."

She regretted her sarcasm as soon as she said it. She heard his thick voice asking, *"Do you want my mouth here?"* She remembered his tone perfectly because she'd been replaying it for four years. Her body flushed with heat and her cheeks stung.

He stared right at her, smug as he reached for a Bloody Mary, opened it with a pop, then drained half of it in a few healthy swallows, never taking his eyes off her.

God, she hated him.

But when he offered her a can of her own, she took it and opened it, taking a big gulp of the tangy, vodka-laced drink to wet her dry throat.

"You really didn't know who I was in Budapest?" he asked in a voice thick with suspicion. He leaned his hips beside her against the back counter so he stared at the water, but she felt his attention on her as though she was under an interrogation light.

"No," she choked. "I would never—Did you know who *I* was?"

"Hell, no." His profile was carved from granite. "Did you tell anyone? Your brothers?"

"Gawd, no. I'm dreading having to explain this." She started to sip, then had to ask, "Did you? Tell anyone?"

"No," he scoffed, sounding as though he'd rather have a bullet dug from his chest with a rusty knife and no anesthetic.

His repulsion was as insulting now as it had been then, making her reach for hostility to hide the fact she was so deeply stung.

"And by the way, my father did not leave your uncle to *die*. Your father and his brother were horrible to Dad while they were all at Harvard. Dad didn't have any love for either of them and didn't even want to be at that party with your uncle. Which is why he was leaving when your uncle asked for a lift. Dad thought he was drunk so he said his car was full. Yes, it was spiteful, but he didn't know your uncle was diabetic and needed his medication. It eats at him to this day that he brushed him off instead of taking him to where he might have got help. But there were dozens of other people there who also could have helped him. It wasn't Dad's fault."

"Yet he had no qualms about keeping up the pressure on my father after that, pushing him into an early grave. Then he came after me while I was burying him."

"Look." She put up a hand. "I was sorry to hear about your father. That must have been a difficult time for you."

"You think?" He snapped his head around to pin her with his hard stare, making her heart stutter and thrum in her chest. "Did you set them on me? Your brothers?"

"*No*. I was trying to forget we'd ever met!"

"I'm sure," he said facetiously. He took a pull off his can and returned his attention to the surf and the falling rain.

"I don't have a say in the business one way or another," she said with a surge of resentment. "My brother is being a sexist jerk about it, if you want the truth. But think about it. Your father accused mine of *murder*. Dad has had to deal with that for decades. So yes, it was tasteless of him to go after WBE when your father died, but he felt justified. He said your grandfather did the same to him when Nonno Aldo died."

Dom drained his can and set the empty can in the sink, making her stiffen as the air stirred beside her hip before he resumed his stance against the counter, ankles crossed and arms folded, glaring at the foam washing up the beach.

"How has this feud persisted this long anyway?" she muttered. "My grandmother didn't want to marry your grandfather. Maybe Michael Blackwood should have got over that instead of dedicating his life to making my family suffer?"

"He was insulted that she preferred a *war criminal*."

"Oh, please. Nonno Aldo could be accused of being a profiteer. Maybe. But people do what they have to when times are tough. Your great-grandparents were bootleggers trying to survive the Depression, same as mine. Don't throw stones at Nonno because he sold olive oil and cheese on the black market during the war."

He snorted, unmoved.

"And so what if my grandmother preferred someone else? She fell in *love*. Your family didn't have to steal— yes, I said 'steal,'" she stressed as he shot her a warning side-eye. "They pulled some questionable stunts, cutting the Winslows out of all their shared assets. *That* was profiteering from a war they instigated. Maybe, once they stole everything, they could have let up? There was no reason our fathers should have been involved, let alone our generation." She pointed between them.

For a few moments, there was only the buffeting wind and the rattle of the awning and the heavy patter of rain on the roof. The light was fading, making the shack seem colder than it really was.

"My father and his brother were twins," Dom said flatly. "Dad never got over losing him. He needed someone to blame. To hate." He picked up another can to shake it, but didn't open it, only set it aside with a grimace of discontent.

Something in the dourness clouding his face made her wonder what sort of father that had made Thomas Blackwood.

"Let's look at your ankle," Dom said abruptly.

"Why?"

"I want to play doctor," he claimed with a fake smile.

She knew he was taunting her, but she couldn't help her reaction of both tension and, deep in her belly, anticipation.

The ice pack, which was the instant, disposable kind that she'd snapped to activate when she'd realized her ankle was sprained, had long lost its cooling properties. Now it was purely for decoration so she tried to bring her ankle into her lap.

Dom turned toward her and caught her leg behind the knee, burning her bare skin with his hot palm.

She reflexively tried to jerk away.

"Would you stop?" He scowled at her.

"I can do it myself."

"I've removed one of these before," he assured her and started rolling down the rim of the condom.

"Can you *not*?" She brushed at his hand.

"What?" he asked with tested patience. "I'm trying to help."

"You're getting your kicks by taunting me. I don't like it."

"Just let me see what we're dealing with."

She tsked as she let him work the condom down and off. He let it fall with the ice pack then gently cradled her calf and heel while he carefully tested her range of movement. His thumb lightly explored the faint blue swelling.

"Hurt?"

Only in her chest where an ache of yearning pulsed.

"Not too much," she said huskily, wishing she could cure herself of this intense reaction to his clinical touch.

"Keep it elevated." He propped her foot on the edge

of the front counter. "Is there a first aid kit? We should wrap it."

"I didn't see one. Stop!" she ordered as he started to remove his shirt. "Use a sarong."

"These sleeves are stretchy. I was going to cut one off." He shrugged and shook out a pink-and-blue sarong before tearing it in half lengthwise.

Eve silently promised to pay for whatever they used while they were here, then succumbed in silence while Dom took up her leg again. He began winding the strip of cotton from the base of her toes toward her ankle. Perhaps he *had* played doctor a time or two. He seemed to know what he was doing, keeping the fabric taut and neat despite the tricky bend around her heel.

He was being very matter-of-fact about it, too, which made the tendrils of arousal that wound through her all the more agonizing. When he tucked the tail in and set her foot back on the counter, she was both relieved and swimming in renewed awareness.

"I'm trying to defuse the sexual tension when I say those things." His golden eyes seemed to visibly spark as he met her gaze. The air between them crackled. "It doesn't work."

He felt it, too? That actually made hers worse. She swallowed a protest that would have been a lie while a wicked swirling sensation in her stomach pooled and slid like quicksilver. She stared stubbornly past him, out the window.

He picked up another can, put it down.

"Are you trying to ration our food? How long do you think we'll be here?" she asked with alarm.

"I'm trying not to get drunk enough to make a pass at you," he said through his teeth.

She clenched her hands around the edge of the counter, aware of how her outstretched leg left her thighs open.

"You don't even like me."

"Yes, I know that, Evie. But *this*—" he waved at his crotch "—isn't listening."

CHAPTER SEVEN

SHE AVERTED HER GAZE, MUTTERING, "Quit calling me that."

"Evie? Why?"

"Because it implies we're more familiar with each other than we are."

His hoot of laughter cracked the air like a gunshot.

"Would you *stop*," she implored. "You're behaving like a child."

"No, you are. Budapest happened, Evie. Walk out of every restaurant in Manhattan just because I'm there. Tell people you don't know me and look right through me. I don't care. It doesn't change the fact that we turn each other on. Or that I hate it as much as you do." The bitterness in his voice was an insult.

But she knew exactly why he was being so acrimonious. She resented him for still enthralling her after all this time. She despised him for making her feel more during the dispassionate wrap of her ankle than any other man had ever made her feel with French kisses or romantic gestures.

And she was so *tired* of feeling stuck and frozen. Rebuffed. Denied. She was stunted by her experience with him because he had been the first and only man she had wanted to have sex with. He had taken her to a height she hadn't known existed then plunged her abruptly back to earth before abandoning her altogether.

She'd never recovered. It wasn't even a matter of courage when it came to other men. She simply didn't want them. She only wanted *this* man. She feared that would never change and that filled her with despair.

"Well, I'm not going to have sex with a man who is involved with another woman so…" She said it as much to forestall any ideas that might crop up in her own mind as his.

"Cat and I aren't involved," he muttered.

"Oh, please. You're her date for a wedding."

"Because the timing worked with my takeover of the resort in Airlie Beach." He was staring dourly toward the water. "My sister has been trying to set us up for a while. I had dinner with her twice before this. We're not sleeping together. Either," he added with quiet significance, alluding to her arrangement with Logan.

That shouldn't make a difference, but it did. There was no obstacle of other people that would have kept her from sleeping with him. Now there was only a potent silence that thickened with sexual tension.

"So what?" she blurted. "We have sex just to get it over with?"

"Possibly the sexiest invitation a man has ever received."

"Oh, go to hell, Dom! You just said you hate that you feel this way. You think that was the romantic sentiment I've been waiting for?"

She immediately wanted to bite back her words,

thinking they were too revealing. She braced herself for some arrogant, sarcastic remark, but he only expelled a grim curse.

"We're like cats in a cage, aren't we? We're going to keep swiping at each other until it happens." He didn't even turn his head to look at her, but he seemed to cast out a net that snared her.

She felt his proximity. She refused to look at him, either. She was fearful he'd see the tears of frustration standing in her eyes.

Outside, the clouds had turned sooty and thick. The wind was gusting hard enough to pick up the awning and make the shack rock on its pontoons.

"Do you have more condoms?" Dom asked gruffly. "If you don't, that will end this. I *cannot* get you pregnant."

A pang hit deep in the bottom of her heart while a fearful excitement filled her lungs.

Lie, she told herself. *Just say no.*

"Two. They're in my bag."

"You couldn't lie?" he asked with exasperation, twisting his head around to glare at her.

"You could simply not use them," she suggested with a bat of her lashes.

A wild flash of lust glinted in his eyes, one that seemed very excited by the idea of naked sex.

"I always use them," he said in a voice that dropped several octaves so it abraded her skin as he spoke. "And *you* could say 'no,' Evie. Say it," he commanded.

She stubbornly sealed her lips and lifted her chin in challenge.

"You're such a pain in my ass." He reached for her bag where it was lying on the floor and passed it to her, holding onto it when she started to take it. "It would only be sex, Eve. Once. We get it out of our system, then we never tell anyone. We don't talk about it. We never see each other again. This isn't the start of something."

"You're saying that as if I want it to be." She noted that he called her Eve when he wanted to impress the gravity of his words upon her.

She took the bag and brought it into her lap, realizing he was doing it again, making her offer him the condoms as a tacit demonstration that this was her choice.

She dug around, brought out a protein bar. "Still hungry?"

"Not for that." The grit in his voice was making her skin feel too tight to contain her. She remembered that voice all too well.

"You have to tell me you want this, Evie."

She found the condoms, two squares stuck together, and offered them.

He didn't take them. He clasped her wrist and said, "You're shaking. Is that fear?"

"No." She wished the helpless pang in her voice didn't make it so obvious this was desire. *Yearning.*

He lifted the bag off her lap to set it out of the way, then edged into the space between her outstretched leg and dangling calf, pushing her thighs farther apart.

"If you want me to stay on my side of the shack, say so." He waited a millisecond before he clasped her hips and dragged her to the edge of the counter so the placket of her shorts was flush to the hard ridge inside his.

A squeak left her.

He might have breathed, "Last chance," then his hand was clasping her ponytail to drag her head back while his mouth came down on hers.

Lightning struck again, strong and sharp enough to hurt. Eve moaned and his arms wrapped around her, almost reassuring before they crushed her. She wormed her arms out of the space between them and up around his neck, then opened her mouth wider beneath his.

No soft seduction here. They picked up where they'd left off in Budapest, kissing as though the other held the last drop of water available on earth. He cupped her head and kept her where he wanted her as he angled his mouth across hers and delved for all the secrets of the universe. He stole and plundered and gave. He poured heat and passion into her. Want. Feral, angry, desperate want.

She absorbed it all with a groan of delight and dragged his shirt up, trying to find his skin. He wrenched it up and off, then pulled her T-shirt over her head. Her bikini top was a tug of two strings, then it also fell to the floor.

His wide hands shaped from her waist up her rib cage, covering her breasts in heat. His mouth dragged from her lips to her neck, heading down.

"I want to give you a collar of hickies," he said against her throat.

"You can't," she moaned.

He lifted his head long enough for her to see the bitterness in his gaze, then his thumbs dragged across her nipples and he was kissing her again.

She wrapped her good foot behind him and levered

herself almost off the counter, balancing on her tailbone as she rubbed and rocked, inciting them both.

Or so she thought until he drew back, expression remote and harsh.

She dropped her hands to the counter and inched herself more firmly onto it.

"Don't lose your nerve now, Evie. We're getting to the good part." He released the button of her fly and lowered the zip, then clasped the waistband of her shorts with two hands. "Lift."

Heart slamming with a sense that she was doing something very bad, she did as he ordered, letting him drag away shorts and bikini bottoms in one go.

She'd been here before, naked while he was still half-dressed and fully in control. She licked her lips and looked for the condom, but he dropped to his knees.

"Like it was built for this," he said with guttural satisfaction. "Like you were. No, keep your leg up like that. I want you right on the edge. Hold on, Evie. Hold on."

He draped her good leg over his shoulder so the contact with his skin burned the back of her thigh. He blew softly across the fine hairs protecting her mound. She twitched and wriggled, but he wrapped his arm behind her hips, not letting her retreat as soft kisses made her thighs twitch, trying to close.

"If you want me to stop, say so."

She couldn't tell if he was mocking her reaction or being sincere. She could only bite her lip and close her eyes as he nuzzled closer. Her flesh was so sensitized and swollen with anticipation, she couldn't speak.

Please, she thought. *Please*.

Without any hurry at all, he painted a slow wet stripe against her inner lips, then again, with more pressure. Deeper.

She groaned. And shook.

He rumbled a noise of satisfaction that she barely heard over the sheets of rain and the crash of surf and the rattle of the awning in the keening wind. As the storm closed in and the day turned to dusk, her world shrank to this, the clever play of his tongue on her most intimate flesh. He brought his hand into the game, delicately parting her, fondling and adding to the sensations so she was nearly arched right off the counter. She pressed her head to the wall behind her, vaguely appalled at how uninhibited she was being, but she had yearned for this for four years. She needed it more than she needed air.

Why was it him that did this to her? Why? Why was he so perfectly skilled at swirling sensations through her like a tornado, teasing her and drawing her up and up into a greater storm of pleasure. Climax beckoned, glowing, expanding.

He gave her inner thigh a juicy, openmouthed kiss then stood.

"Don't stop," she panted, hearing herself beg and hating herself for it.

"I told you I wanted you right on the edge," he said with a cruel grin.

Her stomach clenched and, for one second, she thought he was doing this to her again. That he'd wanted to bring her to this point of flagrantly offering herself so he could reject her.

But he picked up a condom and tore it open with

his teeth. He pulled the drawstring on his shorts at the same time, dropping them. He wasn't wearing underwear and his thick erection sprang out, ready and hot as it brushed her thigh.

"It's time." He efficiently rolled the condom down his length.

It was past time. It was the only time.

"Help me. Show me you want this," he urged, guiding his tip against her aching flesh.

She did, bumping her trembling fingers against his, touching the steely shape of him, exploring briefly then catching at his shoulder as he notched the wide dome of his head so he could penetrate her.

The pressure increased. She tensed, nervous.

"Hurt?" He flashed a frown up at her.

"No." It didn't. Not really, but it was more profound than she had expected. She wanted to cry, she had waited so long for this. And she had always thought that lovemaking would fill her with a flood of love, but she hated him. Didn't she?

Not right now. Not when he said in a voice that was almost gentle, "It's okay. I won't let you fall." He took a firm grip of her thigh. "Tilt your hips."

She did and the thick shape of him slowly filled her, stretching and forging his way in until he was, as he'd promised in Budapest, buried to the root.

She couldn't breathe. She could only hold onto his shoulders and press her open mouth against the side of his neck. She swore she could feel his heartbeat inside her. Her abdomen began to shake. A symphony of contractions worked through her pelvis and loins and she simply *lost*.

She felt his jolt of surprise, then his arm locked low behind her tailbone, securing her exactly where she was. His other hand cupped her neck while he covered her mouth with his own, drinking every cry and moan from her lips as he pulsed his hips, holding himself deep inside her while subtly riding her through the shudders of her climax.

Was it supposed to happen like this? He wasn't even thrusting. All he'd done was arrive inside her and she fell apart. She could have wept, she felt so overwhelmed and helpless. So completely at his mercy.

"I'm starting to think they're going to find us like this," he said in a rasp, scraping his teeth along the edge of her jaw. "Because if that's what I can expect while I'm here, I'm never leaving."

She was still shivering in the aftermath, leaning weakly against him, trying not to sob over how powerful that had been. He kissed her once. Twice. Bordering on tender as his mouth traveled into her neck and across her shoulder while his caressing fingertips teased along her spine and rib cage, then grazed the underswell of her breast.

"Lean back."

She did, not wanting to lose the warmth of his chest against hers, but she braced her hands behind her.

He trailed his touch across her belly and down to where their flesh was locked. His caress was sure and intimate, but light and frustrating as he avoided the spot that would provide the sharpest sensations. Then he brushed the knot of nerves that was still so sensitive she gasped in a mixture of pleasure and discomfort.

"Mmm." She jerked and he did it again. The thickness of him filling her amplified everything, bringing an immediate flood of heat.

"Mmm," he mocked. "You like that." He circled his thumb, avoiding, avoiding, then skimming across in a tease.

She gasped again, accusing, "You're mean."

He dragged his gaze up from watching the play of his thumb. "When it's necessary. Tell me if I'm too rough."

Her heart lurched, but he was rubbing her own moisture against the swelling bundle of nerves at the top of her sex. She bit her lip and arched in reaction, starting to need more of that. Starting to think she needed that for the rest of her life.

Her movement shifted him inside her, promising the friction she hadn't known she desired. His free hand braced her hip as he withdrew in a sensual drag before returning in a slow, deliberate penetration that sent delicious shivers through her nerve-endings.

A small cry of joy escaped her.

This was what it was about, she realized as she splayed her hands behind her, holding herself still for his steady thrusts. This was why there were eight billion people on the planet. This was what everyone was chasing, this sense of being made from gold dust. Of being made for this. For him.

She gloried in the pace he set, layering sensation upon sensation into her. They were folding time so it was compressed and stalled and they could be right here, like this, forever. Like ancient life trapped in amber.

"Evie."

She dragged her eyes open to see his eyes were glittering through the fading light, his cheeks dark, his teeth bared.

"It's me." He lightly pinched her nipple. "I'm the one doing this to you."

"I know." Did he think she was fantasizing about someone else? He was her entire world.

"Good." He set his hand on her lower back and brought her all the way off the counter before he began to thrust with more power.

She grunted in surprise and clasped onto him.

She was bathed in fire, open and defenseless, but safe. Even as tension wound through her, even as she wanted to claw his back for the release he was promising, and even though she knew he resented this as much as she did, she knew they were in this together. That made it better than okay. It was wrong and messy, but perfect.

The rain had cooled the shack, but they were both sweating. They were sticky and clinging and making noises as though working hard.

"Don't stop," she cried as climax danced tantalizingly close, yet remained out of reach, like a star at her fingertips. "Don't stop."

Now he did get rough, shifting to hold her tighter as he thrust with wild, barely couched power. She loved it. She had needed to know she could wreck him as thoroughly as he wrecked her and she could feel how he was shaking and about to shatter.

"Come, damn you," he ordered.

She opened her mouth against the crook of his neck and bit him. Not hard, just hard enough for him to feel her teeth.

They detonated. She didn't know whether it was him or her that hit the culmination first, but they were thrown into the abyss together, screaming and shouting with pleasure. He kept thrusting and the edge of the counter cut into her backside and her ankle bumped something sending a zing of pain through her, but none of that mattered.

Only *this* mattered. The feel of him buried deep inside her, pulsing against her internal clenches. His arms were locked around her and the slam of his heart was against her breast and pleasure radiated through her whole body.

It was a glorious disaster.

CHAPTER EIGHT

DOM THOUGHT HIS orgasm would never end. The hammer-like throbs rang through him, taking forever to slow and fade before becoming latent pangs and twitches.

His arms and legs were trembling with exertion, but he waited until he felt himself slipping out of her before he clumsily made sure she was balanced on her foot. He secured the condom and withdrew, wrapped it in a napkin and tossed it into the bin under the sink.

Then he walked out into the lashing rain, still shaking and soft in the knees.

It was rude, he knew, to exit in silence like that, but he didn't have a word in him. He was too stunned.

Had it been worth the four-year wait? Quite the opposite. He resented that lost time, which was a ridiculous reaction. That was like saying he wished he'd tried heroin four years ago. He shouldn't have tried it *today*.

He walked naked into the crashing surf, then dove into the bracing water, only realizing as he came out that that was also stupid. He could have been stung by jellyfish or carried away on a rip current into the dark ocean. The beach had been deemed safe earlier in the day, but there had also been a hundred people here looking out for each other.

Where the hell were all those good people when he was taking an even bigger risk with his life? If this affair ever got out, both of their families would come after him. Evelina Visconti was absolutely off-limits, taboo and forbidden.

Which had to be the reason that had been the most incredible sex of his life. By a long shot. That, and breaking such a long dry spell.

He knew, though. Deep down he knew it had been like that before he'd known who she was. That's why he'd obsessed over her for the last four years. That's why he hadn't had sex with anyone else. It had to be her. That's why, like a rube fresh off the turnip truck, he'd fallen for the "We'll do it once to get it out of our system" rationalization.

When the heavy rain grew too unpleasant to bear, he made his way back to the shack and used the last light of dusk to find a bottle of wine from one of the crates he'd stored between the pontoons. He'd rather have the Scotch he'd mentally earmarked, but he really would do something stupid if he split a bottle of that with her.

He stepped inside to find her dressed in her shorts and shirt. Her complexion was ghostly in the upturned flashlight of her cell phone. Her ponytail was tidy once again, her profile unreadable as she prepared plates of food.

"Your clothes are there with a towel." Her elbow pointed in a vague direction toward him. "The tap works. I don't know whether the water is potable or how much there is so I only used it for washing. I'm drinking bottled."

"Are you sure the food is edible? Something smells off." Astringent. He set the wine on the counter and stepped into his shorts, ignoring the beach towel and T-shirt. One look at her and he was already too hot inside his own skin. Better to stay clammy and uncomfortable.

"I used some disinfectant."

"On yourself or…?"

Her hand faltered, then, "It's under the sink if you need it."

What a pair of comedians.

"Glasses?" He took up the bottle and realized it wasn't a twist-off. "And a corkscrew?"

She handed over both, then took a gulp of what looked like a freshly opened can of Bloody Mary.

"Are you all right?" He was disturbed by the way she was avoiding his eyes.

"Of course."

"Evie—"

"We said we wouldn't talk about it." She met his gaze for one flat second, mouth stretched into a mean-ingless smile.

Maybe she was having as much trouble processing their lovemaking as he was.

"But you'll tell me if I was too rough," he said gravely.

"I'm fine." She gulped again. "My ankle was hurting so I had another ibuprofen."

"Sit and put it up. I can finish that."

"I'm done. I was just fussing." She shifted a caddy of condiments out of the way and sat on the front counter, setting her back next to the window this time, using the pile of towels and sarongs as a backrest. When she propped her ankle, her outstretched leg was more of a closed gate than an open one.

It was also a more convenient position for her to reach the food, but he felt deliberately shut out by her body language and was irritated with himself for taking umbrage over it.

He poured out the glasses and handed one across, giving the small banquet a proper review as he did.

She'd used the remaining half of the torn sarong as a tablecloth. The pickles and crackers and canned fruit were arranged as beautifully as any thousand-dollar plate he'd ever seen. She'd even found some pistachio nuts and some kind of dip.

"The hummus is from a packet. I used bottled water to make it."

"It looks good." He could have eaten all of this himself. It had been hours since breakfast and he'd carried roughly a hundred and thirty pounds across the island before working up an appetite with her.

She was hungry, too. They attacked the food, not speaking again until there were only a few olives and a lick of hummus left.

"Oh. Dessert." She leaned to dig into her bag. "My protein bar is chocolate-coated."

He snorted. "I thought you were going to offer me the other condom."

The look she sent him made him want to bite his tongue. Or hers, now that the air took on an erotic vibration.

"Yes, I want to use it," she spat with resentment. "Damn you to hell."

"Oh, I'm quite sure that's where we're headed." He snapped out a beach towel, wafting it onto the floor. Then he stepped across to gather her up and take her down onto it.

"Dom!" Eve snapped awake in the secure spoon of his body. His solid chest warmed her back. His hot thighs were bent behind hers and his heavy arm weighed against her waist. There hadn't been any other way to sleep in this narrow space down the middle of the shack. As night had fallen, he'd closed the awning, she'd set down fresh towels and sarongs as bedding, and they had crashed harder than the surf.

Now the floor was shifting beneath them.

She urgently tapped his thigh, trying to sit up and find her phone on the counter above her, but his arm tensed, locking tighter than the safety bar on a roller coaster as he drew a long breath, pulling himself into wakefulness. She blinked her eyes wide, but couldn't see a thing in the pitch dark of this unknown hour. She didn't think they'd slept very long, though.

"What's wrong?" he murmured.

"I think we're floating."

"We are. It's okay." He roamed his hand down her front, ironing her more firmly into the hollow of his sheltering body. "It's high tide. There was only a short beach when we arrived. Remember? That's how he gets this thing onto the beach. It's anchored to concrete blocks underneath. I saw them when I put the booze down there."

"Oh. Okay." She relaxed. Mostly. Because now his hand was petting her thigh, fingertips tracing the seam where her legs were pressed together. He was hardening against her butt cheek.

"That means he'll likely be back in twelve hours to retrieve it," he added.

"We don't have a condom," she reminded, voice growing unsteady with arousal.

"I know," he grumbled and brought his hand back to her stomach.

"We could do other things." She rolled to face him.

"Hell, yeah, we could." He pressed her beneath him and kissed her with urgent, dark passion, invading the recesses of her mouth in a reclaiming of territory he'd conquered only a short time ago.

She met the electric dance of his tongue with her own, greedily taking all that he was willing to give because they had less than twelve hours.

"Stand up," she urged when he started to part her legs.

He did and she used the darkness to hide her inexperience while she learned how to take him in her mouth and pleasure him in every way she'd ever read a man enjoyed.

He seemed to enjoy it very much. He swore and hissed in shaken breaths and his thighs were like iron beneath her hands as she stroked them. When he hit his release, his jagged cries were both triumphant and vanquished.

Then, while she was still glowing with inordinate pride at delivering him so much pleasure, he lay on his back and arranged her in a most unseemly position to return the favor. It was the most sinfully erotic experience of her life on top of a night of generous caresses and life-altering orgasms.

That really should have exhausted their libidos, but the chuckle of a kookaburra woke her to predawn light and the quiet of a blown-out storm.

Dom was already awake. His erection pressed insistently against her backside. As she drew in a waking breath, her breast shifted in the hand that cupped it.

"Your nipple is hard. It's been driving me crazy, wanting to play with it while I waited for you to wake up." He skimmed his hand down and discovered she was already wet.

She moaned with something like relief, shifting her leg so it rested on his, parting her thighs so he had more room to caress into her tender folds.

He groaned with appreciation and opened his mouth against her nape. "Once more? I'll pull out."

They shouldn't. It wasn't just the risk of pregnancy. It was who they were. This was supposed to be an inoculation against wanting each other, but she feared it was only going to make this incessant pull between them stronger.

"Unless there's something more to worry about?" He shifted his hand to her stomach. "I get checked regularly."

She couldn't bring herself to admit that she had never been tested because she'd never been with anyone before last night. She hadn't told him that and doubted she ever would. She wouldn't have the opportunity. They were never going to see each other again. Not if they could help it.

She turned her face into the crooked arm that was her pillow.

"It's okay," she whispered. "I don't have anything to worry about. I can take a pill once we're back in civilization, to be safe."

"Sure?" he asked in a gratified growl even as he drew his hips back and guided himself between her thighs, seeking.

"Yes," she breathed, arching to accept the press and penetration that sealed them together one final time.

He swore and clutched his arm hard around her a moment, sounding breathless as he said, "You feel incredible."

The lack of latex made it more intense. It wasn't just the heightened sensations, though. It was the intimacy. The naked danger. The morning light that took away the fever dream aspect and made it real.

How would she bear never feeling like this again? She would suffer an emptiness for the rest of her life, yearning for him.

She had him now, though. In this moment, she felt divine.

He moved lazily, fingertip stroking through her folds again. She braced a hand on the cupboard in front of her, holding herself still for his easy thrusts.

She was glad he was behind her. This was so good, tears were pressing against her closed eyelids, wetting her lashes. Her longing for this to last forever rose along with her arousal until both were acute. Before she realized it was happening, she broke with a cry.

"Greedy little Evie," he said against her ear, teeth catching at her earlobe while he pumped. "You just can't get enough, can you?"

Her sheath was still fluttering around his intrusion. Her nipples felt bruised under his caress. Her whole body ached from the nonstop lovemaking and the abbreviated sleep on a cold, hard floor. Her ankle throbbed like a migraine and she was tender where he penetrated her.

But he wasn't wrong. None of that mattered. All she wanted was for him to skim his touch down again and reawaken her desire. She pushed back, inviting deeper, harder thrusts, behaving lewdly because she couldn't help herself.

"Me, either," he said, pulling out long enough to bring her onto her hands and knees before him. "This really is the last time." He returned and she pushed back with a groan of welcome.

The surf was at their doorstep when Eve rose and put on her bathing suit and went for a cool, cleansing swim. Dom joined her, also wearing his shorts, as though there were any eyes here to see them beyond each other's.

As though they hadn't seen and touched and tasted every inch of the other's naked body last night.

They barely spoke, barely looked at each other as the glare of midmorning light forced an end to the madness. A reckoning.

A *wreck*oning, Eve thought with irony, as she lowered to sit on the overturned milk crate that had been washed up to the sand a small distance from the shack.

She drank in the paradise of powdered sand and sunlight glinting off turquoise waters and rip curls of foam edging ever closer to her feet, as inexorable as reality. She was stranded with the last man on earth she should want and she half hoped they wouldn't be rescued. She would rather live out their life as castaways.

Dom waded around to join her. He carried two bags of potato chips, her protein bar, and offered her a cup of—

"Coffee?" She sniffed, then sipped. It was terrible. He'd made it with cold, bottled water and it was black, but it was better than none. "Thank you."

"You cooked last night," he said drily.

It was such a domestic thing to say, as though they were a couple who took turns cooking for each other, it brought a hot scald of wistfulness to the back of her throat.

What are we going to do? she wanted to ask, but she already knew. Nothing.

His profile was rugged and remote, his jaw shadowed by stubble and his eyes hidden behind his mirrored lenses. It was not the face of someone who thought their upcoming separation was a problem.

"There he is," he said.

She shot her gaze to the water and saw the flash of a tin boat reflecting the sun. The last thing she felt was relief.

"I realized I had forgotten my sunglasses at the lookout," Dom said cryptically.

"You're wearing them."

"Because I went back for them. That's when I found you limping up the path."

He was feeding her their talking points.

"I went to the spit on impulse," she added. "After leaving Logan barfing on the beach."

"Really?" His mouth curled with amused contempt.

"I caught my foot on a root and twisted my ankle." It was true.

"Our slow progress back here meant we missed the last boat. We spent a sleepless night in the shack, but otherwise we're fine."

Sleepless. She caught back a ragged chuckle. "It's always best to stick as close to the truth as possible."

His mouth stayed in its cynical curl.

"Can I really trust you not to tell anyone?" The raw, searing sensation in her chest wouldn't subside.

"Can I trust *you*?" He was still looking out to sea, not giving her the merest smidge of comfort with that harsh profile.

"Yes." It was untenable that she had trusted this man with her body, with her life even, given how their families regarded each other, when she didn't know how to trust him otherwise. Yet here she was. Alive. Unharmed. So sexually satisfied, she was kind of stupid with it.

But changed, too. Not by sex. By *him*. By the fact they continued to have something between them and always would. Now they had two memories. They were a part of each other's history that couldn't be erased.

"I don't want anyone to ever know I let you…" Her voice dried up as he finally looked down at her. His glare seemed to pierce the mirror of the lenses so she felt it like a pin that poked through her and held her in place.

"You didn't let me do anything," he said in a grim tone. "We did that together."

She turned her hot gaze to the boat bearing down on their cove. The sound of its engine was growing louder.

"I know," she admitted in a small voice. "I just wish it had been anyone but you."

Dom snorted, muttering, "Same," before he waded into the lapping waves, meeting the boat as it cut its engine, but continued to drift closer.

The voice of the astonished operator carried across the water.

"Mate. You two been here all night?" He stammered that he'd been told everyone was off the island.

"No harm done," Dom assured him. "We helped ourselves to what we needed. Bill me for the alcohol that was ruined by the tide."

"I can cover the costs," Eve said when they came ashore. "It was my fault."

Dom shook his head once, abruptly, as though she had offended him.

That was pretty much the last thing they said to each other. While he helped the young man collect everything and secure the shack for towing, Eve combed the beach for any litter that their party had missed yesterday.

When the tide was high enough that the shack was floating, Dom boosted her into the boat. She watched the empty beach grow smaller as they motored away. Their tryst was over.

CHAPTER NINE

IT WAS LUNCHTIME when Eve was dropped at the eco-resort.

She was dying for a long, hot bath and a long, undisturbed sleep, but she had promised Dom she would see first aid. She got her foot rewrapped and they gave her a pair of crutches. She then gave the manager of the resort the story they'd agreed on. The resort hadn't organized the day trip so they weren't liable, but the manager was horrified all the same. He said he would review procedures to ensure nothing like it ever happened again.

Eve made her way to her suite, dreading bumping into wedding guests and having to explain her injury. That would only lead to even more awkward explanations. Hopefully, Logan wouldn't even be here—

He was here. She heard his voice on the terrace. Ugh.

Expecting he was on the phone, Eve pecked out the door to say, "Hey, Logan—"

He was in the hot tub with Cat on his lap. They jerked apart and Cat leapt to the stairs, emerging naked as she hissed at him, "You said she *left*. That it was over."

"I am leaving. Oh, gawd." Eve hurried into her room

and clumsily got her suitcase opened onto the bed, then started throwing things into it.

Logan came in a half minute later, belting a hotel robe around his dripping body. "What are you doing here? I thought you left yesterday."

"I was stuck on the island overnight." Thankfully, the first aid attendant had also given her fresh painkillers which were starting to kick in. Not that she was hurt by Logan moving on within hours. She thought it was sitcom-level hilarious, especially given what she'd done last night and with whom.

Their being here gave her no chance to shower and catch her breath, though. She packed willy-nilly while Logan stood in the doorway and Cat hovered behind him.

"I thought Dom ghosted me," Cat said. "I called his hotel. They said he wasn't there."

"Is he even still alive?" Logan joked lamely.

"It was an uncomfortable night, but we're fine," Eve said mildly. "Would you call the bellman to carry my luggage? I have a flight booked."

She didn't, but ninety minutes later, she was on a chartered flight to Brisbane where she checked into one of the Visconti properties. She spent the rest of the week ambling from her king-sized bed to a pool lounger to pampering treatments in the spa.

She didn't turn on her phone, not wanting to see whether Dom had reached out, which he hadn't, she learned, when she was on her way to New York. She very nearly shut the thing off again when she saw the number of texts from her family, all outraged that she'd thrown over Logan and spent a night alone with Dom.

She sent one quick text to Nico, fueled by her anger over the way he had deliberately held her back because he had consulted *Logan* about her future, not her. It would be a long time before she got over that and forgave him.

As for her parents, she put off responding to their outrage until she was home, only realizing as she arrived at the building on Madison Avenue how embarrassing it was that she still lived with them. They spent most of their time on Martha's Vineyard now that her father was retired so remaining in her childhood bedroom—which had been redecorated three times since she'd been an actual child—in the penthouse apartment had always seemed practical, not immature. She worked in Manhattan so it was convenient, but it probably contributed to the way her entire family still saw her as a child.

Boy, did they ever, she thought dourly, when she came off the elevator to find her parents waiting for her, tapping feet and already wagging fingers. Nico, was here, too, wearing his most smoldering expression.

"I'm moving out," she informed them, hoping to take them by surprise, which she did.

"What? When? Why? Where are you going?" her mother responded in breathy panic.

"I don't know yet. Thank you." She smiled at the doorman who'd brought up her luggage for her. He sent her a "good luck" look and exited.

"What the hell is going on with you, Eve?" Nico asked.

"Did you get my text?" Six words from an old song

had been all she'd needed for her resignation letter. "That's all I plan to say to you for a while."

"You're such a child," he muttered. He was twelve years older and unbearably arrogant.

"I'm not *your* child, though. Even if I was, how *dare* you ask a man I barely know whether I'm going to be too pregnant to work for you? Go to hell, Nico. Go all the way to hell, then go a little bit past it so you're completely out of my sight."

"Evelina," her father said in a dangerous rumble.

"No, Papà. He disrespected me first. This is about my working for him for *four* years and him not once giving me the challenge or opportunities that Jackson and Christo have had at my age. The only reason he's doing it is because I'm a woman. That is sexist and *wrong*."

"The Offermans are an important connection. You threw his proposal in his face then spent a night with *that* man?" her father railed. "Nico has a right to be angry. This is a bad look for the entire family."

"Logan didn't propose," she scoffed. "It was a job offer for domestic service. But you're right, Papà. I'm so very sorry, Nico, that you had to go through the terrifying ordeal of hearing that your sister rejected a man you shook hands with once. She was stranded on a remote trail on an uninhabited island in the Pacific and could have been stuck there for days before someone found her, might even have died, but *that's* not important. Refusing to give up her life and uterus because *you* think she should is the real anguish she's causing you."

"This is why I don't give you more responsibility. You have the temperament of a toddler," Nico bit out.

"Calm down," her mother insisted. "Eve, you're tired. Does your foot hurt? Come sit down."

Eve didn't move. She glared at her brother, then her father's stony expression, then her mother's pinched mouth.

"You all think I'm being hysterical, don't you?"

"Selfish," Nico provided. "We all act for the good of the family. Except you. Because you think you're special. Like Nonna."

Eve realized she was shaking. Her heart was pinched in a vise and all she could think was that she might have been able to comply with an arranged marriage eventually, if she hadn't slept with Dom. Now she knew what she'd be missing and it would make any other man's touch repulsive to her.

She picked up her purse and opened the door.

"Evelina! Where are you going?" her mother cried with alarm.

"I'll let you know when I get there."

Dom wanted to hate her, but he couldn't. He wanted to *forget* her. But he couldn't.

Not when he and Nico were once again playing a game of chicken over a property in Miami.

Eve had nothing to do with it. The timing of Nico's bid made that impossible, but Dom still wanted to believe she had something to do with it.

Why? Because it would prove she was thinking of him? That he was as far under her skin as she was under his?

Even if he was, Eve wouldn't resort to asking her

brother to deliver a message in such a cryptic way. She wasn't afraid to confront someone directly. He'd seen it more than once. He'd felt the smack on his ass, even.

Plus, asking her brother to exact revenge would necessitate revealing why. She wouldn't do that. They'd agreed on a statement labeling their night a misadventure, nothing else. It had been released into a heavy news cycle, burying it. Like the first time they'd trysted, this was their little own secret and, for some reason, Dom liked that most of all.

What was he, nine? He didn't convey messages by decoder rings and peer at diary entries and share secrets under the covers. He didn't share anything with anyone. Ever. He didn't need special connections. He barely tolerated the required relationships of work and basic social fabric. He'd spent his whole life learning to live at a distance from the rest of the world. He liked it that way. It was comfortable.

But he knew so many secrets about Evie now. Intimate ones, like how soft her mouth felt around him when he stood like a lighthouse in the dark, feet braced and hands clenched on either side of the narrow aisle of the shack while she rocked his world.

Then there were the intriguing tidbits Cat had shared with him when she'd come to his hotel. Dom had planned to use the light scandal of his night with Eve as a clumsy excuse to cool things off, but Cat had sheepishly confessed where she had spent the night and with whom.

She must have had a guilty conscience about it because she'd spilled a few of Logan's confidences. As much as Dom had appreciated the information, he'd also realized Cat was a gossip. They definitely hadn't had a future so that was off his conscience, at least.

"Sir?"

There were eight people at the boardroom table behind him, waiting for him to decide whether to increase his bid against Visconti Group while he, yet again, had spiraled into making love with Evie.

"The clock is ticking on our ability to counter," someone else said. "It's already been three weeks. Visconti Group has it locked in unless—"

"I know." Nico had put funds into escrow to secure it.

Which wasn't why Dom was stalling on matching and exceeding his bid. He was suffering a pinch of conscience.

Cat had revealed that Visconti Group was overextended. If Dom wanted to topple the first domino on what could spell the beginning of the end of Visconti Group, he would let Nico have the Miami property. According to Cat, they couldn't afford it.

Dom had been working toward a moment like this for four years. It was the culmination of three generations of bloodthirst. He could hear his father's voice shouting at him to, "Pull the trigger."

Because all his father had ever wanted was revenge. Suffering. He'd thought causing someone else to hurt would somehow make his own pain stop.

No. Despite the attacks he'd suffered through the years at the hands of the Viscontis, Dom knew that crushing his father's enemy wouldn't do a damned thing to fill up the empty spaces inside himself.

He needed to do something else.

"I want to speak with Eve." He turned to confront a sea of confused expressions.

Someone leaned to the person next to them and murmured, "The one in accounting?"

"Evelina Visconti," Dom clarified with exasperation.

"Really?" They all sat taller and looked warily at each other.

"Um, sir?" A hesitant hand went up. "I'm not sure if this is relevant, but when I was doing my research, I noticed she's no longer on their org chart."

"Why?" Because of him?

A startled shrug.

"Find out where she is," he ordered. "I want to speak with her."

Four days later, Dom was vacillating between livid and sticky nausea when he walked into the Miami hotel that Nico Visconti wanted so badly.

It was showing its age, definitely not worth the price Nico had driven it to, but location, location, location. The view from the penthouse was exceptional.

Nico Visconti turned from the windows when Dom entered. He stiffened.

"What the hell are you doing here? I was expecting Perez," he said of the current owner of the hotel.

"I asked him to set this up. Where's Eve?" Dom's staff had delivered the disturbing news that she was quietly missing. Her family didn't seem concerned, but she hadn't been spotted by paparazzi or photographed since Australia.

"Why?" Nico narrowed his eyes.

"She's no longer with Visconti Group. Why?"

"Why do you want to know?"

Good God, they were never going to get anywhere.

"Did it have anything to do with our being stranded that night?"

"You have an exaggerated sense of your own importance." Nico looked at his watch, likely to appear patronizing and dismissive. "Why?" he asked again, gaze sly as it came up to meet his. "Is there a reason I should have fired her? Did you sleep with her?"

Dom had prepared himself for that question.

"Would you excommunicate her for that? How medieval of you. Especially when the grapevine has it that she's saving herself for marriage." Thank you, Cat, for that nugget. "Do you really think she'd break her vow for *me*?" Dom offered his best poker face. "Or that I'd tell anyone if she had? I hear the last man who claimed he had slept with her walked away with a broken nose."

"Because he was lying. My brother knew it. That was years ago," Nico muttered.

"So where is she?" Dom pressed.

"Why?"

Dom's temper started to slip, but he had a flash of memory of her saying, *My brother is being a sexist jerk.*

"You don't know, do you?" He couldn't help a smirk of dark amusement. He knew exactly how irritating it was to be ignored by Eve. "Who can tell me where to find her? Your mother?"

"Do *not* talk to my mother. No one in my family wants to talk to you," Nico said impatiently. "I'm already tired of it." He started past Dom toward the door.

"Wait." Dom pushed his hands into his pockets and rocked on his heels. This was it. Once he took this step, he couldn't un-take it, but he'd been going around and around in his mind, trying to find another way. There wasn't one.

"I want to propose marriage."

Nico froze beside him.

Dom braced for anything, a sarcastic, *Me?* A thrown punch...

He got a scoffing choke. "Are you on drugs? I'd rather throw you off this building and spend the rest of my life in prison than call you my brother-in-law."

"Why?" Dom asked with genuine curiosity. "Do you ever talk about the feud? With your father? With any of your family? We never did." Dom shook his head, not waiting for an answer. "Talking to Eve was the first time I even imagined there was another side to the story my father had told me about my uncle. All I knew growing up was that I was supposed to hate your family. Making the Viscontis miserable is simply what we do, like celebrating Thanksgiving and running hotels. Aren't you tired of it?"

"What's the matter, Blackwood. Are you feeling the pressure? You can't afford this place so you came here to cut a deal that might soften the sting?"

"Oh, I can afford it, Nico. Can you? Does your father know how overextended Visconti Group is?"

Nico's poker face was good, but not impervious. There was the tiniest hint of a flinch in his right eye.

"Eve was supposed to marry Logan to get you out of trouble, wasn't she?" Dom was repeating what Logan had told Cat. "Offerman was a lousy bet on your part. Eve had zero interest in him and he spilled your money troubles to *my* date while they were wrecking his bed."

Nico swore and pinched the bridge of his nose.

"Where's Eve?" Dom asked again.

"You're right. I don't know." He dropped his hand. "She blocked me over how things went with Logan."

"Who does know?"

"Let it go, Blackwood. None of us are going to condone your marrying her. How could we ever trust you?"

"If I wanted to hurt her, I had ample opportunity in Australia," Dom pointed out flatly.

Nico's belligerent stare turned troubled. His mouth tightened and his nostrils flared.

"How bad was it?" Nico asked with gritty reluctance. "That night on the island. Was she scared?"

"It could have been very bad if she'd been there alone. At least I got her to the shack, otherwise she'd have been in the open all night during a storm." Dom refused to pull that punch. "While we were getting drunk, waiting for rescue, she said, 'My grandmother refused to marry your grandfather. Maybe he should have got over it.' She's right. It's time we all got over it. If we don't, who will? Do you really want to consign our children to playing this silly game?"

"We could just put down our swords," Nico said. "Eve doesn't need to be involved."

"True." But that wouldn't bring Evie into his bed, would it? "But you're not wrong about how little trust there is on both sides. We'll both keep expecting a betrayal unless we have an old-fashioned arranged marriage that binds both families into one. The way it was supposed to happen in the first place."

"Is that what this is?" Nico challenged. "Are you setting her up to be left at the altar, trying to settle that old score?"

"God, no. I'm tired, Nico. You've driven up the price on this property to the point it's not practical for either of us to purchase it. But if I don't counter your offer, you're going to be in a very tricky position. Aren't you?"

"So I can have this place or my sister? Is that what you're threatening."

Dom released a beleaguered sigh to the ceiling.

"Why do you even want to marry her?" It wasn't the same cantankerous question. Nico's eyes narrowed as he finally weighed Dom's proposal more seriously. "What exactly happened between the two of you that this is even something you would consider?"

"She's not exactly hard on the eyes." Understatement. "Financially, an alliance between our companies would put us so far ahead, no one will ever catch us. And, believe it or not, I don't relish destroying you. But I *can*." Dom paused to let that sink in. "Now tell me where she is. If she agrees to marry me, I'll buy this place for her as a wedding gift."

Nico's lip twitched into a sneer, but he only asked, "And if she doesn't?"

"Then we'll see."

After a long, unbroken stare, Nico muttered something foul under his breath. Finally, he took out his phone, tapped and brought it to his ear.

"Where's Eve?" Nico asked without any other greeting.

"Call her and ask." The bored male voice was loud enough for Dom to hear it.

"It's important, Christo," Nico said with impatience. "Tell me."

"Where do you think she is?"

"I'm not playing twenty questions."

"Nonna's. *Obviously*."

"Oh. Of course." Nico ended the call. "Our grandmother's villa on Lake Como."

"Give me the address."

Nico did, then said with heavy sarcasm, "Good luck."

"Don't need it. But you do," Dom said and walked out.

CHAPTER TEN

EVE WAS TRYING to go back to resenting Dom. In some ways she did, because she was even more obsessed with him than before their time on the island. It took all her control not to stalk him online or find the number to his head office and try to reach out.

For what, though? They had no future. Putting their family history aside, he was the last sort of man she'd want as a partner. He was too much. Too gruff and dynamic and good-looking and powerful in the ways that he affected her. Her ankle was mostly better, but anytime it gave a twinge, she thought of him throwing her over his shoulder like a caveman, or smirking about removing the condom, or wrapping her ankle so tenderly.

The truth was, she wished she only thought of him when her ankle twinged. It was more a case of thinking about him and feeling a pang through her whole body.

Why? Why *him*?

She feared she would live out her life as a spinster because she seemed to possess whatever instinct or imprinting gene made wolves and geese mate for life. It wasn't love. It was the sort of pair bond that formed as a survival tactic. There was no logic to it. It simply was.

At least, that's what she told herself this infernal reaction was. If she allowed herself to believe this weird bond went any deeper, into liking his dry humor or feeling touched that he'd brought her breakfast, she only felt raw inside because she knew it wasn't the same for him. He'd made it clear their affair was a one-night thing and purely physical. Their parting had been circumspect without even a kiss, the silence since then profound.

Piqued by that and Nico's high-handed behavior and her realization that she was entirely too reliant on her family, she'd come to Italy—where she owned a home. Kind of.

This was the house where Nonno Aldo had brought his bride, Maria, after he had stolen her from her wedding in America. They'd had two years and their first child, Romeo, here before returning to America to bail out the Winslows. They'd held onto this villa and, after losing her husband, this was where Nonna Maria had lived out her golden years.

After she passed, Eve's father had wanted to sell the house because it was small and impractical, not to mention turning into a money pit with age. Eve had a lot of fond memories of visiting Nonna here. She had begged him to hold onto it until she was able to access her trust, at which point she'd got a mortgage and began making it her own.

It *was* impractical, made up of three floors built into a hillside. It was tall and skinny, with small rooms and narrow windows. But it was very cute with its red clay tile roof and its shutters in robin's-egg blue. There was an outdoor kitchen, a small pool, and terraced grounds holding fruit trees and ornamental shrubs that wore autumn colors of scarlet and copper and sunny gold. The view of the deep blue lake was outstanding.

Eve was currently supervising much-needed repairs to a retaining wall while waiting for a headhunter to get back to her when her housekeeper, Odetta, tugged her attention from the work she was surveying below her.

"Signorina?"

Eve turned to see Dom on the terrace above her.

Surprise nearly knocked her over the edge and onto the workmen.

Dom was still gorgeous, the bastard. He wore a light-weight suit in sage-gray. His jaw was shadowed with stubble, his eyes hidden by sunglasses. His hands were in his pockets, his attention seemingly on the view, but she felt his gaze follow her as she crossed the lawn to the bottom of the stone steps cut into the hill.

She took her time climbing them. Questions were tumbling through her mind and conflicted emotions bounced like pinballs in her chest. She couldn't help leaping to worrying that something catastrophic had happened. An exposé of some kind? She'd been staying off socials and off grid, trying to reset her life, but clickbait websites never took a break.

The closer she got, the tighter her skin felt. She subtly cleared her throat, fearing her voice would come out thin and high.

"If you're looking for your next development property, this one is not for sale," she said.

He took his sunglasses off and looked directly into her soul. "It's beautiful."

Her throat contracted around a squeak that she barely managed to suppress. Why did he have to be so damned edible? That mouth. She wanted to press her lips to his and nuzzle the scent in his throat and lean against the column of his body. She wanted to touch him. Feel him. She wanted to take his hand and lead him straight up to her room without another word except maybe "yes," and "more," and "harder."

She turned so she was facing the water, trying to hide her libidinous reaction.

"My grandmother would have spent her whole life here if she hadn't had to go back to America and bail out the Winslows. Will you make coffee, please, Odetta?"

Her housekeeper melted away and Eve waved at the table and chairs farther along the paved stones of the terrace.

Dom didn't move. He tucked his sunglasses into his jacket pocket and gauged the distance to the workmen before asking in an undertone, "Are you pregnant?"

"No." He'd taken precautions, if he didn't remember. Even during that risky third time, he had pulled out as promised. Plus, the timing had been wrong. *And* she'd taken the pill, exactly as she had promised.

Despite how impossible it had been that she could be pregnant, she had still shed a couple of tears when her cycle had arrived as faithfully as tulips in spring. It was yet one more foolish reaction in a list of foolish overreactions this man provoked in her.

"I had to ask. I've been wondering."

"Is that why you're here?" A humorless laugh scraped the back of her throat. "You could have called."

"I don't have your number." He moved to hold a chair for her before taking one for himself. "Why did you leave Visconti Group?"

"Reasons." She shrugged that off.

"Me?"

"No. Family stuff." She frowned pensively at the water. "I didn't tell anyone, if that's what you're asking. We agreed," she reminded him with a sidelong look.

"They might have made assumptions."

"They might have. I didn't stick around to find out. Did your family? Make assumptions?"

"Probably." His mouth curled slightly. "My situation is different. My sisters are from my father's second marriage. We're not as close as you seem to be with your brothers."

"I'm not that close to them. They're a lot older than me. Well," she allowed with a tilt of her head. "I'm close with my middle brother, Jackson. He's here in Italy. I used to stay with him on long weekends when I was at boarding school, only flying home for the longer breaks. He's the one I feel most similar to. Nico is driven and ambitious. Bossy," she summed up with a grimace. "Christo is very laid-back and fun to be around, but kind of impossible because he does what he wants. Jax and I are middle of the road. Sensible. Mostly," she added ironically.

Dom hadn't asked for her to tell him all that, but he seemed to listen intently, then said, "My sisters are all younger. Five of them." He splayed his fingers. "I didn't spend much time with them growing up so I don't really know them."

"Is your mother still alive?" She realized she didn't know.

"She is." He nodded absently. "She's in New York and lives with her partner, but never remarried. It would have affected her support payments. My relationship with her is distant for a lot of reasons."

"Such as?"

"I never fought to see any more of her than my father allowed, which was only a few weekends a year. We don't really know each other."

"Do you wish she'd fought for you?"

"No," he dismissed easily. "We both knew to pick our battles with him. And sometimes I wonder if she saw too much of him in me to make it worth it for her."

"The fact you're here tells me you're not that much like him," she said with an ironic tilt of her mouth. "In what ways are you like him?"

"I'm practical. Determined. I can be ruthless. Like the way I left you in Australia, not looking back. Not even thinking until later that there might be someone else to worry about."

"There isn't," she murmured, stomach doing somersaults above her empty womb. "This is probably the longest personal conversation we've ever had. Did you come all this way for *that*?"

"No."

"What then?" Her voice became a ghost of itself.

The indent at the corner of his lips deepened with humor.

"Oh, *don't*." Her breath shortened. All of her nerve pathways contracted with anticipation.

"I don't know what *you're* thinking," he mocked. "But I came to propose we marry."

If the entire mountainside had fallen down upon her, she couldn't have been more caught off guard.

"We can't. Why would you even want to?" Did he have feelings for her after all? That thought sent her own thoughts scattering. Her heart tripped and thumped, trying to take flight. Adrenaline zinged through her system, urging her to flee because she didn't want to have this conversation. She didn't want to examine how *she* felt about *him*.

"The feud doesn't serve anyone. It has to end," he said simply.

All her ballooning thoughts condensed into a wet sack and fell back to earth. This had nothing to do with her, then. Nothing to do with emotion or attraction or even sex.

A sting of scorn rose beneath her skin. She fought to keep her reaction off her face, but felt as though she wore a stiff mask.

"What makes you think our marrying would end it?" she asked.

"I've spoken to your brother. He saw the advantages."

"You've spoken to Nico." That was a kick in the stomach she hadn't expected. "And he agreed? What do you need me for?"

"This is how warring kingdoms reconcile, Evie. It's one of the few tactics that has worked in every culture for millennia."

Trading women as chattel? She bit back those ripe words.

"Can I show you something?" she asked, working at keeping an innocent expression on her face.

He blinked, puzzled, then curious. He shrugged. "Sure."

She led him through the house and out the front door to the paved pathway that led from the porch to the road above. A pretty wrought-iron rail lined the path. It was covered in grapevines and bunches of green grapes not yet ripe. On the other side of the porch was a small garden filled with Nonna's roses. A few late blooms perfumed the air with lemon and raspberry and vanilla. A silver car was parked on the road above. His, she presumed.

Dom stood beside her, head swiveling. "What am I looking at?"

"My answer." She walked back into the house and slammed the door.

As she turned the lock, she heard his crack of laughter.

She waited, but there was no knock, no demand she let him in. Moments later, there was only the roar of his car's engine.

She left her forehead pressed to the door, bereft that he had given up so easily.

Worry pierced her, too. Had this been a real chance to end hostilities? And she'd allowed pride to take over and throw it away? Maybe she had just poured fuel on a feud that she agreed did need to end.

In a state of turmoil, she made herself go back out to the terrace and drink the coffee Odetta had made while she brooded over yet another proposal that had fallen short of her romantic dreams.

Maybe I want too much, she fretted.

Then, not even an hour later, a florist delivered a unique blown glass vase filled with a stunning arrangement of fragrant lilies and sunny daisies and romantic pink roses. The card read:

I'll pick you up for dinner at seven.

Be ready or I will not do wicked things to you later.

"Oh, you wish!" she cried.

And meant it. Mostly.

Actually, she very much wanted him to do all the wicked, sinful, carnal things they'd done in the Whitsundays. But she wanted that lovemaking to be something *they* wanted. She didn't want it to be something he used to manipulate her, but she was very worried he could.

When she found herself in her closet staring blankly at her wardrobe, she realized she would have to do something she'd been avoiding. She called Nico.

"Eve," he answered abruptly. "Where are you?"

"You know where I am because you sent Dom Blackwood here to propose a marriage *you* arranged. How do I get it through your thick skull—"

"Stop," he commanded. "Listen. You need to know two things."

After a beat of surprise, she lowered onto the tufted bench at the foot of her bed. "Such as?" she asked loftily.

"Dad's health isn't great."

"What?" Her heart lurched. She put out a hand to steady herself while her reflexive ire at being the youngest and always left behind skyrocketed. "Why didn't anyone *tell* me?"

"Mom is the only other one who knows," he said gruffly. "It's his prostate."

"Cancer?" Her heart stopped.

"No. But he's embarrassed to talk about it. They're still figuring out how to treat it, but you need that information as you think about Dom's proposal."

"Because Dad's not immortal? Marrying a Blackwood could kill him, Nico."

"If you decide to marry Dom, I'll talk to Dad," Nico said heavily. "Make him see why it's a good idea."

"It's not a good idea," she cried, letting her pent-up emotions get the better of her. "You and Dom are grown men. Quit fighting. You don't need me in the middle of it."

"We do," he said grimly. "*I* do." He drew a breath, signaling reluctance to continue. "I said there are two things you need to know." This one sounded like a biggie.

"Tell me," she insisted as the silence drew out.

"You know we took a bath when the economy tanked. I made some decisions—for which I take full responsibility," he stressed. "But they were based on the assumption that you and Logan were locked and loaded."

"Oh, my God." She closed her eyes and covered them with her free hand, glad she was still sitting down.

"Mom made it sound like you two were going to happen. *Logan* did," Nico insisted.

"But you didn't ask *me*."

"No. I didn't. I'm asking you now, though."

"Asking me what, exactly?" She dropped her hand and popped her eyes open, but she could only see a blur of blue beyond the window. A cold shiver entered her chest.

"To consider Dom. Seriously."

"Nico."

"He knows he has my back to a wall. This isn't Mom wanting you to marry her bridge partner's son. This ends the attacks and gives us new resources. This is something we need, Li-li."

He hadn't called her that in years. It was the pet name the family had used when she was very small.

Bring your dolls into my room, Li-li. I won't let the boys bother you.

"Are you still there?" Nico asked.

"Yes," she said in a small voice.

"I know I was holding you back at work. I thought I was protecting you from seeing how bad things were. That's how Dad always did things. He carried the worries so no one else had to. Being on the inside comes with a lot of responsibility. Hard choices and heavy burdens. It's not as great as you thought it would be, is it?"

"It's not fair to put them on me now! Like this," she said crossly.

"No, it's not. And I know you like to see yourself as Nonna Maria, living life on your own terms, willing to run away and elope for love, but she left her family high and dry when she did that, Eve. Are you going to do the same?"

She swallowed a sob of helplessness.

CHAPTER ELEVEN

WHEN DOM ARRIVED back at Eve's, he was unsure that she would come to dinner or even open the door. Had that been a tantrum earlier? Or her real answer?

He took the umbrella his driver offered him and moved down the path illuminated by hidden bulbs beneath the shrubs. As he hit the damp fragrance of the rose garden, the front door opened.

Eve's snug satin trousers shimmered above laced ankle boots. Below the mock turtle collar of her cashmere top a wide cutout revealed her collarbone and upper chest. Her long raincoat flared open like a cape as she strode toward him on those endless legs of hers.

She punched his breath clean out of him. He wanted to take a fistful of her black hair and press her to the ground and not come up for air until they were covered in grass stains and smelled of crushed rose petals.

And each other.

She stopped under the umbrella and looked up from the clutch she had just closed.

"You came," he said, because he literally couldn't think of anything else to say.

"I always do. Don't I?" Her pretty mouth, painted

scarlet, curled with self-contempt. She looked to the dark water where lights dotted the far shore.

A cold hand reached into his chest and gave his heart a quarter turn.

"You've spoken to your brother," he surmised.

"I have."

That's why she was here, not because of him or them. Because she knew her family finances were in jeopardy. Why that disappointed him, he couldn't say, since it was a lever he'd pulled to get her address and propose this marriage.

"Where are we going?" she asked.

"Ladies' choice." He kept the umbrella over her as they walked to the car. "I have a table booked at Il Gatto Nero, but it could stir speculation if we're seen dining together." The paparazzi knew that restaurant was popular with celebrities so cameras were always trained on the entrance. "If you'd rather dine privately at my hotel, we can do that."

"Please don't pander to me with the illusion of choice, Dom. We both know I don't have one. The public option is fine."

He waited until they were in the back of his car and his driver had them underway to ask, "What exactly did Nico say to you?" He was dying to reach for her, but he was pretty sure she'd snap in half if he did.

"It's not what he said. It's what he made me realize." She pulled her attention from her side window. "I was very close to my grandmother. She was also the only girl in a family of headstrong boys. Her two eldest brothers had been drafted into World War II and didn't come home. She knew what it meant to be treated as an asset, not a person."

Dom's grandparents had lost brothers to that war, too. It was the reason their great-grandparents had tried to shore up their partnership with the marriage between Michael and Maria, to solidify what they'd managed to hang onto through so many difficult times.

"Nonna didn't want to be treated like a stock, traded and invested by her parents into an arranged marriage, so she defied them and eloped with the man she loved. That always seemed heroic to me. Aspirational. Even though the consequences continue to ripple into my life. I didn't want to see that our family is still paying interest on a debt she incurred. I wanted to believe that her taking a stand meant I could and would be valued for my intelligence and ethics and dedication. That I was a person, not a vessel whose only purpose was to conceive and carry a strategic alliance. These aren't childbearing hips, Dom." She looked right at him as she said that. "Do factor that into your negotiations with my brother when you're attaching a value to this marriage."

Her tone was dripping with bitterness, but all he could think was, Children? He hadn't considered what the reality of a family with her would look like. Some dark-eyed hellion planting her feet and closing her fists and saying a defiant, *No, Daddy*, most likely.

He smirked, entertained by that notion for absolutely no good reason at all.

He waited until they'd wound their way through a sea of glances and murmurs at the restaurant and were seated at a table by the window, wine in hand, before he spoke again.

"Was I your first?"

"What do you mean?" She played dumb, but her eyes flared in alarm.

"You know what I'm asking." He had his answer in the mortified blush that stained her cheekbones and the way her mouth flattened to a pugnacious line while she turned her gaze to the candlelight reflected on the window.

Virginity was not something he prized or even considered much of a thing. By the time he'd hit his first home run, he'd rounded all the other bases dozens of times.

Being her first wasn't gratifying in a possessive, ego-driven way. Well, maybe there was a little of that. He was growing more possessive of her by the minute, but he was doing his best not to be a barbarian about it. No, it was more about what being her only lover told him about her and them.

"You could have knocked me over with a feather when I heard that," he said.

"From *whom*?"

"I put it together from bits of gossip." He shrugged. "The first time I heard that you were saving yourself was in Budapest. To be completely frank, before that, I had never given you a thought. Your whole family was beneath my notice. The late arriving baby sister was never going to be a threat to me so your name was all I knew."

Beneath my notice.

"This is turning into a great first date." She took a hefty gulp of her wine and looked to the window again.

"After I left your room that morning, I caught up with the bachelor party, emerging from their hangover. I asked if anyone had recognized you as a Visconti. They hadn't, but one said he'd heard you were saving yourself for marriage. He knew of a man who'd had his nose broken when your brother defended your honor."

"Jax was demonstrating how it's done," she said with a flutter of her lashes. "So I could learn."

"I dismissed it as urban legend. I had been with you that morning and knew that if I hadn't stopped when I did, we would have had sex. There was no way you were saving yourself."

She sobered and swallowed and frowned at the window. "Can we not do this here?"

"You chose the location," he reminded her.

She threw an aggrieved look at him. "I thought you were only mean when it was necessary."

"This is," he insisted. "You need to hear it. The few times I saw you before Australia, we were in public, but you were always with someone. At the wedding, you were sharing a suite with Logan. Of course, I assumed you were sleeping with him. When you told me you had your own room, I wondered for about half a second if those old rumors were true, but you're twenty-five, Evie. And when *I* touch you—"

"Would you stop?" she hissed, glaring at him. "This is *not* necessary."

"It is. There's a septic little boil between us that needs to be lanced."

"Your love poems need work."

"I want you to understand, Evie."

"Understand what?" Her mouth trembled and her eyes sheened with persecuted tears. "That you have the upper hand? That you can make me do things that are out of character and self-destructive? I *know*. That's why I hate you."

And that was it. "That's why I hate you, too."

She flinched.

He took no satisfaction in it. In fact, concern hit him at her words. It was a worry that had been rubbing like sandpaper in him even before he'd fully grasped that their night together had been her first time having sex with anyone.

"I didn't really believe I was your first until right now," he said gravely. "I wish you would have told me, Evie. If you felt like you couldn't stop me—"

"I couldn't stop myself. Okay? Is that what you need to hear?"

"I need to hear that I didn't hurt you," he said through his teeth, leaning in because they were talking so quietly. "I need to hear that, in future, you will tell me if I do."

The gloss on her eyes thickened. "You're hurting me now. This is *awful*," she told him in a strained, angry voice. "You're putting me on the spot for your own entertainment. How much humiliation do you need, Dom? Tell me the exact degree so I can get there and get it over with."

God, he wanted to grab her and… Not talk. Not have

to find words and admit to things that turned him inside out in the same way they were torturing her.

So he just said it.

"There was no one else for me, either. Not after we met in Budapest. No one interests me, not the way you do. And that made me very grumpy, Evie. *Very.*"

Eve's heart swerved in her chest. Her stomach was already wobbling from his, *"I need to hear that in future..."*

After talking to her brother, her emotions had been all over the place and she'd gathered them all into blame and resentment toward this man because, well, who else would a Visconti target when life was not going right?

"You're lying." She realized they were both angled into the center of the table so they could spike their hot words across the candle at each other. She pressed back in her chair, body trembling as though coming off a wild ride at an amusement park.

"We do a lot of things to each other, Evie, but we don't lie." His mouth was a bitter line that he pressed to the rim of his glass, draining half the contents before he sat back and stared at her, seeming to say *Your move*.

The waiter seized his moment. He rushed in to drop their amuse-bouche before them. With a mumbled handful of words in Italian, he topped up their glasses and hurried away.

Eve took a shaken breath, wondering if the entire restaurant was watching the forks of lightning they were throwing at each other, counting as they waited for the roll of thunder.

"Our marriage will be an alliance that will benefit both our families," Dom said grimly. "I will exploit it in every way I can. I'm not stupid. But that's not why we're marrying, Evie."

She had come here believing she had no choice in this matter and her stomach dipped afresh at the resolve in his statement. At the way he talked about it like it was a done deal.

"We're going to marry because we don't want anyone else." His pinning gaze was impossible to break. "Do we?"

It seemed laughable that he was asking her to speak for both of them, but there was too much acrimony in him for her to believe he was being anything but truthful.

"No," she admitted with defeat. It didn't make any sense, but, "We don't."

He signaled to their server and ordered, "Champagne, *per favore.*"

As the man hurried away, Dom reached into his pocket and brought out a velvet box. He opened it to reveal a stunning oval-cut diamond with a halo of smaller diamonds around it. He set it between them then held out his hand.

Dimly aware of gasps and attention turning their way, Eve set her hand in his palm. The spark between them was almost visible as skin touched skin. She began to tremble all over.

Dom slid the ring onto her finger, sending a sensation like a lasso up her arm to loop around her heart and drag it into his palm so he kept it as he released her.

The ring fit perfectly. She admired it as he rose and came around the table to draw her to her feet. His heavy hand cupped the back of her head and his arm banded possessively across her back. He dragged his mouth across hers in a slow, devastating kiss that rocketed her into a black hole from which she'd never return. The pull was too strong.

Applause broke out as the bucket of champagne arrived.

CHAPTER TWELVE

"WE'LL FLY TO New York tonight," Dom stated when Eve returned from fixing her makeup. "You're a resident there, yes? So am I. We can marry in twenty-four hours."

"Dom." Her knees were so weak, she needed the chair he held for her. They hadn't taken a single bite yet. This was their first date. They might know each other in a biblical sense, but, "We're strangers to each other. We can't marry that quickly."

"I'm not spending the next year listening to threats from our families that they're boycotting our wedding. I'm not giving *you* a chance to change your mind." His eyes gleamed hard as polished bronze. "This won't be an easy sell to either side so we're not going to try. It will be done and their only choice will be to live with it. In harmony," he added with the arid sarcasm she was learning was his trademark.

Eve was trying to rearrange her brain cells to take in all of this. Her brother's call had made it clear that her marrying Dom would solve a lot of problems for her family. Nico hadn't ordered or pressured her to accept Dom's proposal. He had outlined the stakes and *asked*.

He was right about the weight of responsibility, too. It was smothering her.

"What if it doesn't work out? We divorce? That won't be good for either companies or our families."

"No, it won't. We have to make it work, Eve."

He always sounded so grave when he called her that. It was disconcerting.

"What if I can't have children?" She tossed that out as a defense mechanism, since she was running out of arguments.

"Children are not a deal-breaker for me. Your delicate hips are safe if you'd rather not put pressure on them." The corners of his mouth deepened with facetious amusement. "I have a nephew who has the temperament to be my successor at WBE if necessary, but we'll cross that bridge when we have to. I'd like children if you're up for it. I don't see my nieces and nephews often, and they're absolute monsters when I do, but for some reason I enjoy them."

Oh, God. She didn't want to *like* him, but how could she not when he said something like that?

"Do you want children?" he pressed.

"I always thought I'd have two or three," she admitted. "So I could bring them here for the summer and yell at them not to track sand into the house, the way Nonna did with us."

"Sounds idyllic. Any deal-breakers?"

"Love. At least, it used to be." She dropped her gaze to hide how much disappointment lurked within her, then lifted her lashes to meet his cool, flinty expression. "I imagine that sounds immature to you?"

He took a moment to consider his words.

"I hated those four years of abstinence." His voice was hard, but reflective, not assigning blame. "Since the island, I keep thinking it was good that we didn't get together in Budapest. The first time I saw you, I knew you were too young. Not just for me, but for the sort of affair we would have had. I'm glad you have some life experience behind you."

Did she, though? She wished she'd had a dozen throwaway affairs and at least one broken heart instead of carrying fractures in her heart that he had put there. Either way, she didn't think anything could have prepared her for this. Him.

"Don't you want to marry someone you love?" she asked hesitantly.

"I won't say I don't believe in it, but love seems… It comes with high costs. It's as much a weapon as anything else."

"That's not true." Did he really believe that? Why? "Love is a cushion. A home base. A place of safety. Love protects you."

"From what? Meteors? Life is going to impact you, whether you love someone or not. I'll grant you that love can skew how you react to those impacts. In my father's case, his love for his brother set him on a mission of vengeance."

Was that the reason for his cynicism? She was still troubled by the things he'd said about his father in Australia.

"He sounds like a difficult man," she murmured.

"He was." His face closed up, becoming shuttered

and remote. "My mother had the sense to leave him, but my stepmother was forever trying to pull redeeming qualities out of him. Because she loved him. It was painful to watch."

"Painful to be his son?" she surmised.

"Yes," he said with a blink that was a small, unconscious flinch. "He taught me that living without love is easier, especially if it was never there in the first place."

A vast plane seemed to open before her, empty and desolate. She had the sense he was out there somewhere and had the fleeting thought, *I'll never reach him.* An ache arrived in her throat.

"You grew up believing your grandmother running away with your grandfather was a demonstration of love, but for who? Herself?"

"What's wrong with that?"

"Nothing. Just be honest about it. Where's the cushion for her family in that?"

"She was nineteen. She couldn't have *known* your grandfather would react so harshly."

He ran his tongue across his teeth behind his lip, studying her as though weighing whether to say something.

"What?" she prompted.

"I believe my grandfather felt something for her. That's why he was so devastated by her eloping with someone else. I think my father never got over my mother leaving him, which added another layer to his bastardish behavior. Love is not the great, wonderful entity you want it to be, Evie. It's destructive."

She turned her face to the window, trying to hide how

much it hurt that he was reducing her yearning for that emotion into a girlish notion.

"Have you never felt anything like it?" she asked. "A crush? What about the woman you were engaged to? Are you this jaded about it because of her?"

"No," he said without hesitation. "Our marriage would have been advantageous in many ways and she blew it up because I didn't carve out my heart and offer it to her. I have no hard feelings because I had no soft ones." His lip curled. "No, I've only felt anything remotely like a crush once."

Who? A scald of envy, of threat, engulfed her.

"That sexual crush has been torturing me for four years," he continued, voice pitched low with intensity. "I'm determined to turn it into something productive. Otherwise, I'll burn down the world around me. Or *your* world, anyway, like my father and his father before that."

It hurt to hear that she was only a sexual crush to him, and that he felt it was destructive, but his words also sent the unsteadiness of anxious anticipation infiltrating her belly, sending out fingers of tension and ready heat.

"You?" he asked with gentle mockery. "How many crushes have you had?" His eyes narrowed to golden, laser-sharp slits.

"I wish other men interested me," she admitted with a pang of despair. "Women. Anyone. I hate how helpless you make me feel. But I can't devote my life to being your…sex doll. If that's all we have between us, I'll need to find personal fulfilment elsewhere."

"Meaning?" The way his voice dropped to subzero raised goose bumps on her skin.

"Work. I just told you no one else interests me," she reminded him.

Dom blinked, then shrugged with something like impatience, as though this was a topic completely lacking in importance. "If you want to work, work."

"At a real job," she stressed. "Not some lame portfolio picking out wallpaper and cutting cake. Not something that's handed to me like a toy to keep me quiet."

"I'm insulted." He sat back to frown at her. "Do you see me as sexist? One of my sisters is a human rights lawyer. She has joined an organization that sends her to countries where men don't think women should speak, let alone have the level of education she brings to the table. I hate it. I think constantly about how I need to be available to fly at a moment's notice to bail her out of trumped-up charges, but I'm so proud of her, I can't stand it. If you want to work, I won't hold you back. I'm perfectly capable of finding my own dinner if you're not there, barefoot and pregnant, to cook it for me."

"Well, I don't have her level of ambition. If that's the bar she sets, you're going to be disappointed in whatever goals I pursue."

"I'll be happy with whatever makes you happy. I don't want to come home to a miserable wife, Evie. She won't want to have sex with me."

She rolled her eyes and buried her reluctant grin against the rim of her champagne flute. Damn him for being arrogant, truthful, and self-deprecating. For being charming in his crude way.

"We've covered children and work. Do you have a preferred religion? I have none."

"Judging by the way we behave, I don't think either of us do."

That earned her a snort of appreciation.

She shook her head in answer. "Nonna was Catholic, but I haven't gone since her funeral. What about a prenup? We need time for that."

"We'll sign something that ensures our properties remain our own until such time as we've worked out more formal contracts post-nup. You're right. Those negotiations could take months, but if we're already married, that should take a lot of the contention out of it."

"Because Nico needs your money? Dom—"

"No. I know what you're going to say and no, I don't want to wait. We can put off sex until our wedding night, if that's important to you, but I want that night to arrive very soon."

"Are you laughing at me?" Because she hadn't been waiting for her wedding night. She'd been waiting for him.

"I'm laughing at both of us." He reached across the table to still the hand that was nervously playing with the stem on her wineglass. "We've wasted enough time, Evie."

Heaven help her, she felt the same. Even these weeks since Australia felt like time they'd thrown away out of stubbornness and stupidity when she could have had that hand all over her. The mere touch of it was making her tremble with desire.

"All right," she murmured. "Let's fly back to New York tonight."

This was likely to be a disaster, but she was marrying Domenico Blackwood.

By the time Dom's private jet landed in New York, rumors of their engagement had leaked from the restaurant onto the global airwaves. It was midmorning and, since Eve also had her identification on her, he had his driver take them straight to the courthouse to apply for a marriage license.

The law required they wait twenty-four hours so he booked them an officiant for precisely twenty-four hours later. At her request, he dropped Eve at a boutique while he made the rest of the arrangements for their wedding.

It was just a business deal with a side of sex, but an unfamiliar restlessness stalked him until they met again at his penthouse. Then he finally relaxed, which unsettled him in a different way.

Evie was crashing from jet lag so he put her in a guest room—reluctantly—and found his own bed a few hours later.

The following day, he invited his mother and Nico to his penthouse. He didn't tell either of them what was happening so his mother arrived without her partner, perhaps expecting an update on the stock portfolio he managed for her.

"Oh," Kathleen Blackwood said with a self-conscious touch of the pearls when he introduced Eve and explained what was happening. "I would have worn something nicer if I'd known." She was as elegantly turned out as always in a sweater set over a slimline skirt, hair coiffed and makeup flawless. "It was kind of you to invite me," she said as she pressed her cheek to each of Eve's.

"Dom said you were the one person on his side who might actually support this marriage," Eve said with a hopeful quirk of her brows. "And since my own mother isn't here, I wonder if you'd be willing to come zip me into my gown?" She was still in the yoga pants and loose T-shirt she'd put on when she rose.

"I'd be honored."

Kathleen came back to the lounge a few minutes later wearing a smile he'd never seen before. It was somewhere between serene and optimistic. Maybe even, as she found him across the room, pride?

An unsteady sensation hit the middle of his chest, one that made him look impatiently for Evie so he wouldn't have to examine whatever this inner wobble was.

"She'll be out in a moment," his mother said as she squeezed his arm. "You know, given how your father always talked about them, I don't think I could have imagined a Visconti being so charming. She's lovely, Dom. I'm really touched that you chose to include me. I hope this means that… Well, that things can start to heal. For everyone."

The way she searched his eyes caused the wobble inside him to grow worse.

It's practical, he wanted to argue. *Just business. Just sex.*

It wasn't supposed to be an emotional tonic. That was too much pressure to put on either of them.

The elevator dinged, saving him from the sense of walls closing in.

"That'll be Evie's brother." He started to brush past her, but he hesitated and gave her arm a light squeeze. "Thank you for being here. I hope we can all move forward, too."

Nico entered and grew both confused and suspicious when Dom introduced him to his mother.

Evie came out from the bedroom in a gown the color of whipped cream. Its one-shoulder crepe fabric clung smoothly and seamlessly to her torso and hips, flaring midthigh just wide enough for her to walk. Her hair was in a simple knot held with a silver clasp.

Such a jolt of pleasure hit him at the sight of her, Dom could hardly breathe. He'd had a fresh haircut yesterday and shaved this morning. He was dressed in his best suit, but he suddenly wished he'd had time to have a new one made. As much as he wanted this union formalized and finalized—and consummated—he could see the care Eve had taken despite this not being the wedding of her dreams.

It struck him that his sisters had approached their own wedding days with giddy excitement. Eve was very subdued, especially as she came up against her brother's thunderous reaction.

"What the *hell*, Lina?"

Dom held out his hand in a silent command that she come to his side, which she did, but not because she needed his protection.

"What," she said in a mild voice. "You asked me to do this."

"I asked you to *consider* it." He glared at Dom. "Why

the rush?" He snapped a look of fresh shock at Evie. "Are you pregnant? Did you two sleep together in Australia?"

"When have I ever asked you about your sex life?" Evie snapped right back at him. "I really need you to check this sexism of yours, Nico. It's 2015."

"No, it's—" His mouth tightened and her brows went up. "*Are* you pregnant?" he demanded.

"Still none of your business," she said coldly. "But, no. I'm not. Although, people will probably presume that, won't they?" She wrinkled her nose as she looked up at Dom.

"Dad already does," Nico warned. "He called me yesterday when the engagement rumors started."

"What did you tell him?" Her hand tightened in Dom's.

"That you were on your way back to New York and that you and I would come see them today to explain."

"You'll have to manage that on your own," Dom interjected. "We're leaving right after the ceremony for our honeymoon. We can only stay away a week since Evie has a job interview next Wednesday that she can't miss."

"Where?" Nico frowned at her.

"I don't know. Did I miss a call?" She looked up at him in confusion.

"WBE has three executive positions coming available this year. One starts in a couple of weeks, but they could all benefit from your skill set. I'd like you to meet with our hiring team and consider whether any appeal. It's not nepotism." He turned that onto Nico. "Or a continuation of our rivalry, although I think we both operate best with a healthy sense of competition. No, I genuinely think you have slept on her potential. I refuse to make the same mistake. Ah. Here's the officiant," he noted as the elevator pinged once more.

His housekeeper hurried from the kitchen with the bouquet and a broad smile.

"Evelina," Nico said, quiet and urgent. "Are you sure about this?"

She searched Dom's expression. Her dark brows were lowered to a tense, conflicted line as though searching for something in him that he very much feared he didn't have.

When she nodded jerkily, he relaxed.

Moments later, they were repeating the words their officiant provided. The vows were taken straight from city hall, short and sweet.

"Domenico, do you solemnly promise to love, honor and respect Evelina for as long as you both shall live?"

"I do."

"Evelina, do you solemnly promise to love, honor and respect Domenico for as long as you both shall live?"

"I do." Her voice was quiet, but steady. Her hand was soft and warm when he threaded her wedding band onto it.

Dom had never imagined wearing a ring could feel any more profound than wearing a tie pin or a wristwatch. This whole day should have felt as though he was only collecting one more person onto his list of dependents, but he somehow knew that no matter whether that gold band sat against his skin or in a safety deposit box, he was changed by it. Not branded or bound, but linked to Eve in a way that defied logic or description.

"By the power vested in me, I pronounce you married. You may kiss!"

As Dom took her in his arms, she tensed slightly and flashed an apprehensive look up at him. Anxious tears threatened to dampen her lashes.

Don't let my brother see what I'm like with you.

He heard her voice in his head as clearly as though she'd spoken the words aloud.

Dom angled so his shoulder blocked Nico's view of her. He cupped her cheek and pressed a kiss across her trembling mouth, holding there in soft reassurance. Her passion was for him and him alone, not something to be put on display for anyone else to witness.

But even in that brief kiss, need and desire danced toward urgency. Her lips pulled at his with invitation, tempting him to linger and feed the fire.

Soon, he promised, keeping his arm around her as they broke apart and smiled for his mother's snapshot. Moments later, the paperwork was finished. Dom texted his assistant to release the statement they'd agreed upon and carried their luggage into the elevator while Evie changed into travel clothes.

Nico rode down with them, muttering that he hoped to reach their parents before they saw the headlines.

Thirty minutes later, he and Eve were in the air, flying south. They each held a glass of champagne, but she was worrying her bottom lip with her teeth.

"What's wrong?" he asked her.

"My parents. I should have gone with Nico." She worried the edge of her phone with her thumb.

A surge of possessiveness had him wanting to dismiss whatever guilt or obligation she might be experiencing, but he made himself say, "Are you feeling strongly enough that I should ask the pilot to turn this plane around?"

"No," she said on a sigh. "Dad will need some time to cool off. Mom, too. She's been planning my wedding since she heard the words, 'It's a girl.'"

He let out a subtle breath.

"I'll foot the bill on the reception. Tell her to go whole hog."

"Ironically, it's always been a family joke to warn me not to elope like Nonna Maria. A joke, but not really," she clarified with a crooked smile. "Now I have, but instead of running from a Blackwood, I'm with one."

"Are you regretting that?"

"No," she said promptly, then grimaced slightly at how quickly she'd said it.

Which was cute. Endearing.

"No," he repeated as he picked up the hand wearing both his rings. He set his teeth against her bent knuckle. Her gaze hazed exactly the way he liked to see it.

"What are you thinking about, my pretty little Evie?"

"Um…" Her lashes quivered as she watched the play of his lips against her twitching fingers. "That…um…"

It was like a switch, this thing between them. It took absolutely nothing to flip it and once it was on, it was *on*. But he made her say it. He wanted her to acknowledge it. He needed her to. The small beast inside him needed to know she was exactly as helpless to it as he was.

"I've…um…" Her cheeks flushed with shy color. She glanced to the flight attendant in the galley before leaning closer to whisper, "I've always wondered how one joins the mile-high club?"

"Oh." He was absolutely addicted to her when she was both carnal and curious. It turned him on like nothing else. "It's a very exclusive club. You need a personal invite."

"By someone who's already a member?" Her tone grew piqued.

Uh-oh. "Not at all," he said smoothly. "You could definitely ask me to become a member with you."

"Well, then. Consider yourself invited." She unclipped her belt and rose.

CHAPTER THIRTEEN

EVE'S THOUGHTS AND emotions were all over the place. Part of her did want to turn this plane around and run home to where she was safe. She had *married* Dom Blackwood, essentially still a stranger to her. How had she thought this was a good idea?

Oh, right. He only needed to skim away her light jacket, fingertips grazing her bare shoulders and upper arms and she was suffused in heavenly vibrations. He slid the zip on her simple sheath down her spine and she shimmied to help him drop the navy crepe over her hips to drop it to the floor.

Turning to face him, she began working on the buttons of his shirt. He'd removed his tie and jacket when they had boarded and pulled the tails of his shirt free of his trousers.

"Evie." He caught her urgently working fingers into a single, firm grip, halting her. His other hand found the side of her neck. "I've just realized." He waited for her gaze to meet the glow in his. "You're mine."

Her stomach pitched at the magnitude of that statement.

"Are you mine?" she asked shakily.

"This ring says so, doesn't it?" He tilted the hand that was gently crushing her tangled fingers, making his gold band wink. "We're going to spend the rest of our lives doing this. Why don't I show you I'm capable of seducing my virgin bride?"

After everything they'd done on the island?

"That look." A rusty chuckle rattled from his chest, then his expression sobered. He cupped her face in two hands as though she was precious and worth gazing upon. "Every time we've come together, I've leapt on you like you were my last meal. I would have been so much more careful if I'd known."

"It's okay." Her voice rasped from the bottom of her throat, cheeks stinging as she laid bare the truth. "I liked it."

"I know you did," he said throatily, making her want to pinch him. "I like that you match my appetite so closely, but let me have this." He dropped a soft, soft kiss on her lips. A quest and a promise, one that made all the small defenses she managed to keep up against him shift and waver on their foundations.

I don't know you, she wanted to say, but she was learning that he was capable of gentleness. He was almost tender in the way he reverently framed her face and brushed his lips across hers again and again, coaxing her to open for him. To cling and encourage and invite. To deepen the kiss by degrees until his kiss was all that she knew. All that she needed—to be held by him. Connected and suffused in these lovely, shimmering waves.

Her hands began to roam beneath his open shirt, exploring the warm planes and rough-smooth textures of his chest, his taut skin and the fine hairs and his pebbled nipples.

He sucked in a breath, abdomen contracting. He deepened their kiss, releasing her face to drag her into a more sensual embrace. The brush of his hot chest and crisp, open shirt against her mostly naked torso made her shiver.

Helplessness was stealing over her like the shadow of night. She would lose herself to him, she realized. When it came to enemies, he was the most insidious kind. He turned her against herself, weakening her from within.

She tried to take some measure of control by drifting her hands down to his belt.

He caught them and had them manacled behind her back before she'd realized how easily he could do it.

"I said slowly, Evie."

A catch of alarm went through her, then her breasts felt the heat of his gaze. They swelled in her bra, hardening from only a look. Her nipples stung.

He watched his own finger slide under the navy blue strap, drawing it to fall off her shoulder.

Her breaths were uneven, her nervous system vibrating with excitement and anxiety as she tested the strength of his grip. Her movement shifted her against the ridge of his erection.

His gaze was molten gold as he flashed her a look.

She held his stare and pressed her hips harder into his.

"You're the one who always breaks first," he taunted as he ran his hand over her ribs and around to her spine, casual in his claiming of her exposed skin. Proprietary in the way he pushed his hand into the back of her cheekies and palmed a soft round globe.

"You like controlling me," she accused.

"I like touching you," he corrected and slid his hand around to the front of the midnight-blue lace that covered her mound. "I like seeing what my touch does to you. I like feeling it."

She bit her lip, trying to keep her sob trapped in her throat, and closed her eyes as though she could hide from the fact that her folds were damp and swollen with yearning for the fingertip that delved and explored.

"Look at me," he commanded quietly.

Her eyelids felt too heavy to lift, the exposure too raw. It hurt to let him see how much pleasure she derived from something so small as the light play of his touch against her most intimate flesh.

"Tell me when you're close." His voice had dropped into a low, hypnotic tone that centered her world on the glitter in his gaze and the lazy caress that drew her closer and closer to a dangerous precipice.

"Kiss me," she begged in a whisper.

"Not yet. Keep looking at me."

This was so flagrant! At least on the island, she'd had the dim light of the shadowy shack to hide behind. He was forcing her to let him see exactly how thoroughly he dismantled her with hardly any effort whatsoever. It was a show of dominance that was both disconcerting and a ferocious turn-on, making her squirm under the struggle.

Her heart was thundering, her skin burning. Her body grew taut with ever deepening arousal as he dipped and withdrew, caressed and circled and dipped again. She was caught in a slipstream of pleasure, arching ever tighter, breaths reduced to aching gasps of urgency.

"Please." She licked her dry, panting lips, so close she wanted to scream. "Please, Dom." She closed her eyes in bliss as the white-hot pleasure rose like the tide, about to consume her.

He withdrew his hand.

She snapped her eyes open to see the amused, gratified look on his face.

"You're being cruel!" She struggled against his grip and he released her, only catching at her arms to steady her when she staggered drunkenly.

"It's a *game*, Evie."

"It's our *marriage*." She was shaking, wildly aroused and furious and reacting to the enormity of being tied to him when he was so arrogant and imperious. "If I can't trust you here—" She waved at the bed.

She suddenly wanted to cry, which felt like the greatest humiliation of all. She pushed the heels of her hands into her eye sockets, devastated in a way she couldn't articulate.

His clothing rustled. It sounded as though his belt hit the floor.

She dropped her hands to see him sprawl onto his elbow on the bed. He wore nothing but his wedding band. He was ridiculously beautiful, all lean muscle and tanned skin except for that pale strip across his hips, accentuating that he was unabashedly aroused.

A fresh wave of weakness attacked her along with a

fresh flood of heat. She hugged herself, sliding her bra strap back onto her shoulder as she did.

"I said I'm yours, didn't I?" He was wearing his most remote expression, but for some reason it caused a pang of empathy in her chest. "Take what you want. Or walk out if you're that mad."

She bit her lips together, fearful they were quivering like a child's. "I don't know how to handle this." She threw that at him in a ragged accusation, as though it was his fault that she reacted like this. "The way you make me feel is too much, Dom."

"I keep telling you, we do this to *each other*. We have to stop hating each other for that." He held out his hand. "Come here."

She hesitated, but if she walked out now, the nascent threads of trust between them really would break. She had made this bed and longed to lie in it. With him.

She skimmed away the last of her clothes and joined him on the bed. He was still rock-hard and it only took the brush of his hands on her to reignite her own passion, but she curled into him on instinct, seeking more than sex. Comfort. Shelter.

He closed his arms around her and pressed his lips to her hair. "You're safe here, Evie. Always. I promise you that."

Physically, yes. She believed him. Emotionally? Not yet. Maybe never, but that wasn't his fault, either. He might play erotic games, but he didn't play mind games. He wasn't making empty promises to lead her on.

That was the part that really scared her, though. She didn't know how to cope with the way he made her *feel*. She was afraid that she could fall in love with him. Maybe already was and she wasn't even sure why. Because of the way he made her feel when he set adoring kisses on the side of her face? He was still a Blackwood. A stranger.

Yet he shattered her defenses with the warm crush of his mouth and the scintillating pleasure of his touch innocuously tracing the rim of her ear.

She abandoned her misgivings and turned her face into his throat, rubbing her cheeks against his skin like a cat sharing scent, marking him in her own way. She stretched out so she was long and lithe against his tensile strength and danced her fingertips down his spine then traced the line between his tight buttocks.

This time when he drew a sharp breath and caught her hand and pressed it to the mattress above her head, she only gave a moue of contrition and kissed the point of his chin.

"I'll be good," she promised.

"You're always good." He kissed her, once, twice, then shifted down to collar her neck with kisses. His lips trailed down, covering her breasts reverently, pausing to catch each of her distended nipples and rolling them with his tongue. He kissed her all over, down to her lurching abdomen and across her hips. He rubbed his lips against the inside of her thigh, breathing hotly, "So soft."

The pinprick joy of his kisses moved to her center where he easily brought her back to the fever pitch of a moment ago. When her muscles were strung wire-tight, she clutched her fist in his hair and moaned, "Dom."

He lifted his head.

"I'm not on the pill," she told him.

"What does that mean?" He opened his mouth on her inner thigh and sucked. Hard. "Should I wear a condom?"

"Only if you want to. And why do you *do* that?" She jerked away from the suction of his mouth against the top of her thigh. It hadn't really hurt, only threatened to, but she would have a small shadow of a love bite there tomorrow.

"If I get you pregnant, that's it, Evie." He rose to loom over her, hard knees pushing her legs apart so he could settle the hot thickness of his erection against her aching loins. "We're in this forever. Do you understand that?"

She nodded, even though she didn't think there was any way to fully comprehend the scope and magnitude of tying her life to this man.

In a single flex and surge of his body, the silken, aggressive shape of him forged into her. He was returned to her. Claiming her anew. The bleak emptiness she hadn't wanted to acknowledge was doused. Eclipsed. She was bathed in a halo of fire.

He muttered something and spared a moment to catch some of her hair and wind it around his fist.

"Evie," he said in a rasp of anguish right before he claimed her mouth with unrestrained hunger. As he began to thrust, she grasped at his shoulders and brought her knees up to cling her legs around him.

With each powerful thrust, he stole a little more of her. Possessed her a little more deeply.

This was what she had been afraid of, but in the

throes of this pleasure, there was no fear, only glorious indulgence. He was driving her toward a wall. Driving them. The barrier might break when they hit it or they might be the ones to shatter. Either way, she was desperate to get there and urged him on with agonized gasps and the cut of her nails and the eager tilt of her hips.

"Evie," he said again. This time it was almost a curse. His heartbeat pounded against her breast and his ragged breaths stirred the hair near her ear.

They weren't going to survive it, but here they were. The world was fracturing and cracking and exploding. Perhaps they flew into the sun. Either way, she was nothing but white light. She and Dom were no longer physical or separate. They were made of the same, singular, eternal energy.

Then ecstasy crashed over her, ripping her breath from her body in a cry of sheer joy. His shout joined hers and the shock waves of his own culmination slammed up against hers.

They clung to each other, sweaty and groaning and lost to the maelstrom.

Eve only had one thought—that this would happen again and again for the rest of their lives.

Eve woke with a start, naked in the wide bed in the stateroom of Dom's yacht. Sunshine and mahogany hit her eyes. A tropical breeze came through the open windows, dancing across her skin where it wasn't covered by the sheet.

She was on her stomach and lifted her head to look for Dom.

He sat slouched against the headboard, also wearing only the corner of the sheet as he thumbed the screen of his phone.

This is my life now, she thought with sweet excitement.

She would fall asleep sated and wake to the sexy vision of his bare chest and sensual mouth, his stubbled jaw and the lazy, possessive gleam in his eye as he slid a look toward her.

"I thought we made vows," she said with mock indignance.

Both of their phones had been blowing up by the time they'd landed in Miami. Eve had spoken briefly with her mother, who was concerned on many fronts.

"Your father is very upset with Nico," her mother had said. "He didn't want you to know about his doctor visits."

"Can I talk to him?" Eve had asked with trepidation.

"He's still in with Nico. Let him calm down first."

She'd then exchanged a few texts with her other brothers, both of them asking if she "had" to marry Dom— implying they presumed she was pregnant.

After that, she and Dom had turned off notifications, promising not to check them until they were on dry land again.

"My purser informed me that my sister is in Jamaica, visiting her husband's family," Dom explained.

"You spoke to the purser like that?" She flicked her gaze to the naked, muscled thigh poking out from beneath the draped sheet.

"He used the intercom, so, yes. I did."

She was falling in love with that laconic humor of his.

Wait. No, she wasn't. She scrambled to catch her slipping heart. Evie, *don't*.

Dom brought his phone to his ear. "I got your message. We're in the Caymans, but we can fly over for the afternoon. Is Ingrid with you?"

The woman's response was muted and puzzled. "No. Why would she be?"

"It was just a question. We'll see you later."

He ended the call, then looked to Eve with an unreadable expression. With a single fingertip, he guided her hair off her cheek and tucked it behind her ear. "And so it starts."

She bunched the pillow under her chest, hugging it. "Who's Ingrid?"

"My stepmother."

"Why were you asking if she'd be there? Are you worried she's going to hate me?"

"She already does."

"Ouch." She scowled at him.

He shrugged off his blunt words. "My father was extremely good at spreading his poison. She always sided with him, feeding into it. It was the only way she could be close to him. That led her to believe she had some influence or control over the family and WBE, but it was an illusion even before Dad died. My marriage forces her to accept that. She won't take it out on you, though. I won't allow it."

Eve studied his dispassionate expression, thinking of his mother who had been near tears when she had zipped Eve's gown.

"This gives me so much hope, Eve," Kathleen had said with a misty smile. "He's always been so opaque to me. He learned to keep to himself out of self-defense. I did the same, not realizing I was losing him until he was already gone. But this… I mean it when I say I want the absolute best for both of you."

"What was your childhood like?" Eve asked him. "Did you spend most of your time with your mother or your father?"

A subtle stiffness came over him, one that made her think he was going to deflect without answering the question.

"Neither." His offhand tone sounded forced. "Dad married Ingrid very quickly after his divorce from Mom. Ingrid didn't like me underfoot, but she felt my father's influence was threatened if I spent too much time with Mom so I mostly lived at boarding school."

"Really? How old were you?" She frowned.

"School age." He shrugged. "Seven?"

"That's young to be away from home. Was the school in New York or…?"

"New York at first, then Eton so I can 'talk like this.'" He put on a somber British accent. He leaned to set his phone aside and plumped the pillow behind him. "I didn't mind. Being away was less drama and I made social connections that serve me to this day. I came back to America for high school, Andover, and spent summers abroad. Dad would send me to whichever property would teach me a new language and something about the business. Paris, Madrid, Athens, Tokyo."

It sounded very alienating and lonely. Her brothers

might have called her a pest, but she hadn't been *unwanted*. She'd always known she was loved.

"You must have spent time in Sydney?" she joked lightly. "I heard you say, 'Crikey, mate' the day we were rescued. I was so grateful you could make our plight understood to the locals."

His mouth twitched. "You've missed a career in stand-up."

"There's still time." She rolled away, then pushed her pillows to the headboard. As she sat up beside him, she pulled the sheet across her naked breasts. "Tell me more about your relationship with Ingrid. Why didn't she want you around?"

"Because I wasn't hers," he said as though it was obvious. "That's why I have five sisters. She was trying to produce a contender for the throne."

"Are any of them not?"

He snapped his head around to give her a frosty look.

"You were the one who gets offended at being called a sexist."

"None want it," he clarified. "Freda is a lawyer. I told you about her. Astrid and our middle sister married young, likely to get out from Dad and Ingrid's thumbs, though they'll deny that. They're dedicated homemakers. The youngest is an artist. Glassblowing, mostly. She's very talented. My second youngest is brilliant in some ways and struggles in others. She works directly for me, remotely from her apartment. She analyzes data and does other nerdy things that no one else will touch, but she thrives on it."

"And the nephew who could be your successor?"

"Zeke. Freda's son. He's twelve, very focused and bright. A natural leader. To be honest, Ingrid had her heart set on his ascension, believing she put in enough years with my father that she has as much right to WBE as anyone else."

"That tells me exactly how she'll react to me and any children we might produce."

Ingrid would channel her late husband's antipathy against a Visconti, but she would also see a threat to the tentacles she had already wrapped around the Blackwood fortune.

Judging from the radio silence from Eve's father, Romeo didn't seem to be coming around, either.

"What have we done, Dom? Did we burn down our lives for the sake of a few orgasms?"

"They're very good orgasms, Evie." He floated a caress down her arm and tingles followed like stardust.

"I'm being serious. How is this marriage supposed to build bridges? Did you marry me just to throw me in your stepmother's face?" she asked with a twinge of suspicion.

"You know why I married you." He dropped his hand away.

"Sex." She didn't mean to spit the word out with such contempt, but it seemed such a paltry return for the challenge ahead of them. "At least Nonna married for love."

"Don't be naïve. She married for sex. She didn't want to sleep with my grandfather so she ran away with yours." Dom left the bed and pulled on a pair of board shorts, which was the extent of clothing he'd worn since they'd cast off from Miami four days ago.

A chill settled over her chest.

"It was love, Dom," she insisted. "Not the destructive kind, either." She was still sore about those things he'd said about that. "She did one thing for herself and here I am still paying for it."

"I'm the one who will be paying, Eve." He turned to face her, armor up, battle-ready. "Your brother's situation isn't all due to the feud. Quit playing martyr to history and thank me for bailing him out."

She curled her fist into the sheet, chest pierced by the lance he'd just plunged through her. She really had been traded for a bride price. Her eyes were hot, but she willed the tears not to well and pressed her quivering lips together, refusing to say anything at all.

After a long, charged moment, he muttered, "I need to arrange our flight," and walked out.

CHAPTER FOURTEEN

DOM WAS FEELING prickly and keyed up as he and Eve were driven from the private airfield to his sister's villa.

He wasn't one to navel-gaze and fret about conflict. It was the state he'd grown up in. His father had had a hair-trigger temper, always ready to become combative. Dom had learned to navigate those rough waters the way an experienced kayaker went through the rapids in a chasm. Sometimes you got bumped or bruised, but you always survived it.

So his argument with Eve this morning shouldn't have grated on him, filling him with a sense of *this is bad*. The argument shouldn't have happened at all. He shouldn't have risen to the bait of her dismissing their relationship as "just sex" and snapped at her over it.

What did they have other than sex, though? What did he want from her? He'd been raised to expect very little from those who were close to him. At least, he'd found that was the best way to avoid being disappointed so he typically clung to that strategy, but with her—

"Dom?"

Her small voice dragged his attention to her crinkled brow and the wiggle of her fingers in his too-tight grip.

He didn't remember picking up her hand. He released her.

"Are you worried about my meeting your sister?" she asked.

"No," he said with a dismissive scoff. Astrid was a people-pleaser by nature. He suspected the only reason she'd invited them was because it was the polite thing to do. Either that or Ingrid had asked her to.

The car turned through a pair of open gates and the villa came into view. Dom had never been here so he leaned to admire its architecture of glass and stucco arranged like building blocks that were stacked and fanned out to take advantage of the views offered by its private beach.

Dom came around to help Eve from the car and kept her hand as they walked past a water feature to the double doors.

"Astrid's husband, Jevaun, is a music producer. His father is a development banker, but the rest of his family are in the music industry. His mother is a famous folk singer here."

Jevaun opened the door to them himself. He was dressed casually in a T-shirt and board shorts, feet bare, brown head shaved bald and black beard shaved down to a narrow chinstrap. He held their youngest, Adio, who was slumped against his shoulder.

"Dom." Jevaun thrust out his hand. "Good to see you. Congratulations."

Dom liked Jevaun. He was ambitious, but not in a showy way. His clients were A-list superstars, but Dom only knew that from perusing the awards Jevaun had won. He was far more likely to brag about his kid's new tooth than any of the songs he'd launched to the top of the charts.

"This is Eve—I almost said 'Visconti.' Eve Blackwood. My wife." Damn, that was satisfying.

"Nice to meet you." Eve shook Jevaun's hand.

"Adio." Jevaun nodded at the boy whose head of short, tight curls was heavy on his shoulder. "I need to put him down. Astrid and the kids are outside."

Dom usually only saw his sisters on occasions like weddings or, perhaps, a birthday where he might make a point of taking one out to dinner. He'd seen them more often when his father had been alive, crossing paths with them in the six-story limestone mansion that Ingrid still occupied on the Upper East Side of New York.

He rarely visited their homes so this great room littered with children's toys and small clothes in bright colors was also new to him.

Dom's father never would have allowed so much disarray. Children were to be seen and not heard. If they were seen, they were clean, neatly dressed and stayed in one spot. They didn't run at you wearing paint and glitter, shouting, "Uncle Dom!"

Jayden's wide grin revealed front teeth that were too big for his six-year-old face. The top of his hair was in an intricate pattern of cornrows, the sides shaved up in a fade. His sister, Maya, was four. Her hair was in long braids with neon-colored beads swinging off the ends.

"Mama said we could go in the pool when you got here," Maya said, all big dark pleading eyes. "Will you come in with us? *Please?*"

"And throw me like you did before?" Jayden asked. "Please, please, please?"

"You remember that?" Dom hadn't been in a pool with these kids in well over a year.

"Jay. Maya. Can we please say hello properly first? This is your new Auntie Eve." Astrid came up behind the children, blond hair in a ponytail, freckled face clean of makeup. She wore a loose sundress that billowed over her baby bump. "Hi, I'm Astrid." She shook hands with Eve, eyeing her with open curiosity. "This was unexpected news. Congratulations, Dom."

She *hugged* him.

Dom honestly couldn't remember that ever happening and stiffened in surprise.

Astrid's smile faltered as she stepped back before he'd even thought to return her embrace. He caught the flicker of something across Eve's expression, but Astrid spoke again.

"I said we would see about swimming," she reminded the children while setting a quieting hand on her bouncing son's shoulder. "Jevaun's parents said they'd take them if we want adult time. Jevaun can drive them over."

"I don't mind. We brought our suits." Dom glanced at Eve.

She nodded.

"Wash up first," Astrid told the excited children, pointing them to the outdoor shower. "Uncle Dom doesn't want to come out of our pool looking like a unicorn. Jevaun will come in with you, but can I persuade you to visit with me in the shade, Eve?" Astrid waved at a pair of comfortable loungers placed in the shadow of the gazebo. "I'm dying to put my feet up. We have a housekeeper come in for a few hours every morning while we're here, but mostly we try to simply be a family. It's relaxed and messy and makes me appreciate the nanny, let me tell you," she added in a rueful aside. "Let's get some drinks for everyone, first."

Eve started to follow Astrid inside, but flicked a glance at Dom that was vaguely amused, as though she was conveying that she expected an interrogation and was willing to be a sport about it.

Dom watched her go, protective hackles raised, but also something more possessive. A voice in his head protested, *Evie is mine.* He didn't know where it came from. A lifetime of being on the periphery, he supposed.

Which was where he liked to be, he reminded himself, but that exclusion didn't sit as well this time. It was so disconcerting, he made himself move into the pool house to get changed.

"This invitation probably feels like a setup," Astrid said once she and Eve were settled on the loungers watching the men play with the children in the pool. "It is a little. When my sister called to tell me Dom was married, and to who, and that you were honeymooning here, she said, 'You have to invite them over and get the scoop.'"

Eve couldn't help her wistful smile. "I always wanted sisters. I love my brothers, but they're so much older, they've never really felt like confidantes."

"I used to think brothers were just harder to be close to, then I met Jevaun's family. You don't realize how dysfunctional your own family is until you meet one that works. They're so tightly knit, it makes me wish…"

Her troubled gaze fixed on Dom. He was helping Jayden balance on his shoulders before he stood up, launching the boy into deeper water.

Eve waited, but Astrid only reached for the glass of lemonade on the table between them.

"So what is the scoop?" Astrid asked. "Obviously, you two met in Australia. We've all read about that."

"I'm not pregnant. I'll quash that rumor before it starts," Eve said drily.

"Oh, that's too bad." Astrid smoothed her sundress over her bump. "I was hoping for more cousins in our mob."

"It really doesn't bother you, that I'm a Visconti?"

"Oh, I had to place an emergency call to my therapist, believe me." She grinned cheekily. "But it was more about me and my relationship with our father. How is your father taking it?"

"I'll let you know when he starts talking to me again." She grimaced, wishing she was joking.

Astrid made a face of sympathy. "Mom is pretty upset, too. But—Did Dom tell you how Dad reacted when Freda came home pregnant at sixteen?"

"She's the one who is a lawyer? He only told me she has a son."

"Yeah, he's great. I love that little man to bits, but it was a whole thing. Dad threw her out and wouldn't let any of us talk to her, but Dom found her a place to live—a nice place—and bought her groceries and paid her doctor bills and yelled at Dad until he came around.

But that took years. I was kind of shoved into the eldest sister role and there were so many expectations on me." Her brow furrowed with anguish. "I was genuinely terrified Dad would rather ruin Jevaun than let me marry him so I introduced him to Dom and Dom told Dad that he could keep driving his daughters out of the house or he could smarten up. That's his version. I have no idea how it actually went. All I know is that we had a beautiful wedding and Freda was there. So I absolutely support Dom marrying whoever he wants, but I also know that if Dad were still alive, things would be really hard right now."

"I know," Eve said pensively. "And I won't pretend my family are a bunch of innocent victims. My dad and brothers have fueled the fire at different times, but Dom said your father never really got over losing his brother. That it made him bitter and looking for someone to blame."

"That's such an understatement." A sheen came into Astrid eyes as she looked to the pool again. "Dad was so proud of the fact that he had never hit us. That was his bar of good parenting because his father used to give them the belt. But the way he talked to us and things that he did, they were still abusive. Mom was totally codependent, feeding his moods and opinions so he wouldn't turn on her. I've had eight years of Jevaun and counselling and I was still a nervous wreck that Dom was coming over."

"Really? Why?"

"Because he looks and sounds so much like Dad," Astrid admitted in a pained whisper. "But look at him.

My kids think he's the cat's pajamas. They hardly ever see him, but they were so excited he was coming."

Dom was on the diving board, holding Maya's feet so she could do a handstand before toppling backward into the water. He waited while Jevaun boosted her out of the way before he did a flip, making her scream with laughter as his splash swamped her as she clung to the ledge.

"If you're not pregnant, why did you marry him?" Astrid asked. "Is it really just to end the feud? Or something more? Love at first sight? I'm a romantic. Don't hate me."

"I couldn't hate you," Eve said truthfully. Astrid was far too earnest and nice.

But she couldn't look at her, either. All she could see was Dom, four years ago, walking into a club and looking straight at her.

He glanced over now as he came up against the edge of the pool. She felt the same hot arrow pierce her chest.

Yes, she thought. *I think that's what it was.* For her, at least.

"Okay?" Dom skimmed closer, maybe reading the conflicted joy that was closing around her like a fist.

Eve nodded and worked up a brave smile. "I'm just explaining to Astrid that being trapped on that island forced us to talk about how the feud was only causing pain on both sides. I suppose we could have tried matching one of your sisters to one of my brothers…" She was joking to deflect from deeper, trickier explanations around why she had agreed to marry him.

Because I love him.

Astrid seemed to find the idea of her sisters with a

Visconti highly amusing. Her laughter pealed out and the conversation moved to other things.

"That was a fun day," Eve said sincerely as the tender motored them through the dark from Grand Cayman back to the yacht.

"It was," Dom agreed, sounding introspective.

"I was going to arrange a lunch with your mom and mine, to talk about the reception. Astrid suggested I do something similar with Ingrid, so she feels included in the arrangements. She thought that might help smooth the way with her. I wish Dad would get back to me."

Her father's silence, screaming of his sense of betrayal, was eating holes into her gut, especially now that Eve was realizing she'd been in love with Dom for years.

It sounded ridiculous even in her own head. She hadn't known anything about him when they'd met, not even his name. Maybe chemistry *was* what some called love at first sight, but her intense emotional feelings toward Dom were the reason he'd been able to hurt her so deeply by walking away that morning in Budapest. She'd felt *loss*. It had been amplified by the belief they would never have a chance. Ever.

However nascent and illogical that initial infatuation had been, she was learning it had underpinnings of deeper regard. As she came to know him better, she was learning *why* she loved him: because he was patient with children and stood up for his sisters and had overcome what sounded like a really difficult childhood.

She wanted to ask him about that, but a wave of compassion rose in her, one that wanted to hug the boy he'd been—shunted aside and living with the anger of a man his sister was still afraid of. Eve closed her hot eyes, looping her arm across his chest as she savored the weight of his arm across her shoulders. He tightened his hold, snugging her safe and warm against his side while her heart expanded too big for her chest. It hurt to swallow, her emotions were so sharp inside her.

"I shouldn't have said what I did this morning," he said in a low voice. "It's been bothering me all day. It's something my father would have done, trying to put someone in their place by saying something ugly. I don't want that feud between us, Eve. I want it *gone*."

"Me, too," she assured him. "I want us to be like Astrid and Jevaun."

"In what way?" His arm loosened and he looked down at her, expression shuttering.

In love. That's what she wanted to say, but she didn't want to set herself up for a stiff dose of reality so she described the love she'd seen between them.

"They're affectionate and trust each other to have their back. They're a team, especially where the kids are concerned. They make each other laugh."

She heard the rumble of acknowledgment in his chest. A frown of consideration settled on his face.

Was she watching him take a prescription for what she wanted out of their marriage and weigh whether he could deliver it?

She didn't know how she felt about that. It fell somewhere between pandering and endearing and made her wonder if he even knew what love *was*?

"Astrid said—" She glanced at the driver of their

boat, who seemed far enough away not to hear them over the engine. "She said something about how dysfunctional she thought your family was." Eve didn't know if Dom knew that his sister saw a therapist so she skipped mentioning it. "Is that something you believe, too?"

"Yes." No hesitation.

"Have you ever talked to anyone about it?"

"Like who? Astrid?"

"Or a professional?"

"There's no point. You can't change history."

"But you can reframe how you think and feel about it."

"I don't want to talk about my feelings. I don't want to feel them." He didn't sound disparaging or even self-deprecating, only resolved. "This is what I'm doing about the past." He gave her another squeeze. "That history is over. We're moving forward from here."

In what way exactly? she wanted to ask, but they arrived at the yacht. And, because it had been several hours since they'd done so, they went directly to their stateroom to make love.

CHAPTER FIFTEEN

Dom had Nico come to his head office for their first meeting on the post-nuptial contracts. It wasn't meant to be a power move. Eve was down the hall, finishing up her meeting with his hiring team so she would join them momentarily.

While he had her brother alone, however, he said, "Your father is ghosting Eve. It's starting to upset her."

"He's angry with me, not her. And they're away, sailing in the Galapagos with friends. It was planned ages ago, before this and—" Nico let out a hacked-off sigh. "Dad's had some specialist appointments lately that haven't gone as well as he'd hoped. That's confidential," Nico added with a warning look. "But it's adding stress to this situation that wouldn't have been here otherwise."

"Understood. But is that why your mother hasn't nailed down a date for the reception?" They'd suggested a date in November before the holiday parties started, but Ginny had demurred, something else that was distressing Eve.

"Yes. Dad has a procedure scheduled as soon as he gets back so they want to see how that goes."

Dom nodded at the assistant who glanced through

the window. She came in with a cart of fresh coffee and trays of fruit and pastries.

"How long do you think this will take?" Nico eyed the food. "I thought we'd agree on the high-level points and let our lawyers work out the nitty-gritty."

"Eve's been tied up all morning. She doesn't really eat breakfast."

"She's been like that since she was a kid," Nico said with a shake of his head. "And she runs when she's stressed so she gets too skinny at times. If that's what she's been doing lately then, yeah." He nodded with approval at the cream-filled eclairs and bagels with cream cheese. He waited until the assistant had left to ask, "She's definitely not pregnant?"

"My assistant?" Dom deadpanned. "I haven't asked. I'm not allowed."

"Eve. Obviously."

"Can I give you a word of advice?" Dom was enjoying this. "Don't ask about my sex life with your sister unless you really want to hear about it."

"This is why I'd rather keep hating you," Nico said without heat and helped himself to a cup of coffee.

Dom wasn't just protecting Eve's modesty. She'd been quite desolate to learn on the last day of their honeymoon that she wasn't pregnant. Dom had been surprisingly disappointed himself, not that he'd shared that with her. He hadn't wanted to make her feel worse, as though she'd let him down or anything. He wasn't even sure why he found the idea of having children so appealing. They'd been fresh back from watching the circus that was Astrid and Jevaun's life, which really was a lot of work, but he kept thinking about Eve saying she wanted what they had. The affection and tag team of parenting. The trust.

And there was something very simplistic about spending time with children. They were so unreserved, wrapping their wiry little arms around his neck, secure in the belief he would keep their head above water. He'd enjoyed watching Eve play a game with the toddler when he woke, holding him in her lap while she used the tail of her braid to tickle his arm and hand and cheek, both of them grinning and giggling.

He wanted to give her that. He wanted to give her everything she asked for if it would make her smile like that.

A sensation of the floor shifting beneath him struck, as though he stood on the tip of a diving board, toes curled on the edge, muscles gathering to jump and flip.

"Here she is," Nico said as Eve came through the door in a whirl of energy that pushed him into the deep end without any grace at all. Just a big, unexpected plunge with an accompanying rush in his ears and a loss of his breath.

"Hi." She hugged her brother very briefly, gaze on the table. "Oh, my God. Thank you. I'm starving." She came around the table to Dom. She clasped his arm and rose on her toes to kiss the corner of his mouth. "Seriously. You're my absolute hero for this."

She took the chair he held for her and began filling a plate from the tray, oblivious to the fact he felt punched in the face for no reason whatsoever. He didn't even know what had happened to him a moment ago. Low blood sugar, maybe?

"How did the meeting go?" Dom asked her as he and Nico also sat.

"Good. I'm leaning toward the London project, but we can talk later about how that would fit with your schedule. Why isn't Dad calling me back?" she asked Nico abruptly.

"They're sailing—"

"Oh. The Galapagos. Right. Mom was looking forward to that. Tsk. Okay, we can cover family stuff later, too." She waved. "You two talk business while I eat."

They did, discovering quickly that they were mostly on the same page, even sharing the same concerns over how much they should integrate the two companies.

"You should put together a task force," Eve interjected. "Jackson would be a good lead, which might not be your first choice, if you're worried about bias," she acknowledged in Dom's direction. "But you want someone with attention to detail, who will keep you out of trouble with the FTC, but could find where the alignments would reduce costs versus where the individual branding is an advantage."

Dom looked to Nico.

Nico knew exactly what he was thinking and said, "I don't hate the idea."

"Of Jackson?" Eve looked up from her plate of fruit.

"Of you." Dom sent a patronizing glance at Nico. "This is what happens when you hold someone back. They lose sight of how much value they bring to a given situation."

"*Me?* I'm biased on both sides," Eve argued.

"Exactly," Dom said. "You'd want what's right for the whole, not one or the other. We'd need committees on both boards to provide arm's length oversight."

"Agreed. In fact, we can allocate a budget and let her run it as a consultant so she's not on either payroll. She could hire her own team to evaluate and make recommendations." Nico nodded. "But no more digs about how I can't see her potential."

"Sorry, Dom." Eve's hand came to rest on his. "Needling my brother over his colossal shortsightedness falls under my purview."

"I defer to your expert knowledge on that front." He shared an amused smirk with her and pinched her fingers into his palm.

"Are you two having fun?" Nico asked with heavy sarcasm. "*Would* you be interested in running a team like that?"

"You know…" Eve nodded. "I think I would."

Eve was settling into something that felt a lot like marital bliss.

She hadn't started working yet. She had hired an agency to work out the structure of her consultation proposal and they were being absolute sharks about it. That was earning her good-natured complaining from both Dom and Nico about the cost, but there was rueful approval in those remarks, too.

The negotiations on the post-nuptial agreement were going smoothly, but the reception date was still in the air while she waited for her parents to return from their trip.

In the meanwhile, Eve had lunch with Ingrid and two more of Dom's sisters. Dom had wanted to come with her, acting so protective she couldn't help loving him a little bit more, but she'd finally reminded him, "I can stand up to you, can't I? Are you really worried I can't handle her?"

With a grumble, he acknowledged Eve was a "pretty tough cookie" and let her go alone.

Thanks to Astrid paving the way, it hadn't been too painful. His sisters were stilted, but Eve had the sense Ingrid's presence kept them from being as welcoming as they might have been if she hadn't been there.

Ingrid came across as cold and self-centered, but she also struck Eve as someone who lived in fear. Fear of being irrelevant, fear of losing what she had, fear of being judged. Eve left feeling sorry for her and the children who had to bear the weight of all that insecurity.

At least Ingrid had promised to put together a guest list which told her she was willing to attend. It was small progress, but progress all the same.

Finally, Eve's parents returned home. They stayed in the Martha's Vineyard house for a couple of nights to recover, then came into the city the day before her father's procedure was scheduled.

Eve invited them to the penthouse for an early dinner. She kept the menu light, conscious of the fact her father would have to fast before his surgery tomorrow.

"You're nervous," Dom noted, stilling her hand as she tremblingly shifted a butter knife two millimeters—as though its position would affect the outcome of this meeting.

"This is a lot bigger than Daddy's Little Girl marrying the town bad boy. I know you're ready to let bygones be bygones, but I'm not sure he is and that puts me in the middle."

"I would never ask you to choose between us, Evie." He rubbed her arm through the soft wool sweater she wore over tailored blue trousers. "You asked me once how our marriage would bridge the divide. You're it. You're the bridge."

"I hope that doesn't mean I get walked all over," she said wryly.

"No." He cradled the side of her face in a warm hand. "You're one of those feats of engineering that everyone marvels at because they thought it was impossible."

"Your poetic turn of phrase is a marvel," she teased, starting to lean into him, lifting her smiling mouth to invite a kiss.

The elevator sounded and she abruptly pulled back, then ran her suddenly clammy hands down her hips. They moved to greet her parents as they came out.

"Mom. Dad." Eve hugged each of them, feeling their stiffness as she did. "Have you two ever actually met Dom?"

"No." Her father stared coldly at her husband while he ignored the hand that Dom started to offer. "Nico said this was your choice. Is that true?" her father asked her bluntly.

"Romeo," her mother murmured.

"Yes," Eve answered firmly. "Come in. Let's talk." She waved toward the lounge.

Her father didn't move. He flicked his gaze around and shook his head. "This isn't right."

"Dad. Dom isn't his father. I know you had—"

"You *don't* know," he near shouted, making her jump.

"Let's keep this civil." Dom touched Eve's elbow and stepped forward so she was shielded half a step behind him.

"We're still out of sorts from travel," Ginny excused, earning a glare from Romeo.

"My mother would tan my hide for this." Her father's eyes dampened. "She refused to marry a Blackwood and I cannot believe Nico made you do it instead. We have options, Lina. I don't blame Nico for the mistakes he made. No one has a crystal ball, but he never should have pressured you to fix the problems he created. We'll restructure. You don't have to do this."

"Dad." She felt Dom's hand tighten on her arm. "It's done. We're married. Happily." Mostly.

"Don't lie to me."

"I'm not. I—" She looked up at her husband, not having expected to tell him like this, but she let the words spill past her lips. "I love Dom. I have since the first time we met."

His expression only stiffened further, which put a coil of tension into her belly. His cheek ticked.

Oh, no. He didn't welcome her feelings. A chill entered her chest, one that warned her she'd made a horrible mistake.

"And you?" Romeo challenged Dom. "Do you love my daughter? Is that why you married her?"

Dom took his time answering, jaw working as though he was looking for the right words.

"If you're asking me if I married her as an act of revenge, the answer is no. The feud no longer exists. Not in this house. If you're still carrying it, you should take it elsewhere."

She gasped, as did her mother, but Dom wasn't finished.

"Eve can come to you anytime she likes," he continued. "I told her I wouldn't ask her to choose between us and I meant it, but I won't fight you for her. I won't fight you. Not anymore."

"That doesn't answer my question," her father pressed.

"Romeo." Ginny touched his arm.

"You're really going to stay here?" her father demanded of Eve, eyes wet with outrage and disappointment. "Married to a man who doesn't love you?"

You don't love Mom, she bit back saying.

She was trying to keep this from devolving into something that none of them could come back from. Trying to keep from dissolving into tears when she was being forced to face that her husband didn't return her love.

She was hurt enough that she easily could have gone home with her parents and crawled into her old bed and cried for a week, but that's what an immature version of herself would do. She was a woman who had made a decision for herself that had far-reaching consequences, but she was willing to live with them.

"It's a good match, Dad." That felt like such a weak thing to say in the face of what he wanted for her. She was both shaken and touched that he did want more for her, but, "This is good for both families. You know it is. I can't walk away from it now."

"That's what I keep telling him," her mother murmured. "It's done and we need to accept it."

"You don't deserve her," her father said in quiet thunder at Dom before he turned to press the button for the elevator. It was still there so the doors opened immediately.

"Dad." Eve's heart lurched as he stepped into the car.

"I'll talk to him," her mother promised as she stepped into the elevator with him.

"I'll come to the hospital tomorrow and sit with you," Eve promised her mother while her father looked through her as though she was dead to him.

The doors closed and they were gone.

"Eve—" Dom tried to turn her to face him, but his touch burned past her skin, into the marrow of her bones.

"I want to go for a run. Please?" She pressed against his chest, refusing his touch.

He nodded curtly and released her.

CHAPTER SIXTEEN

WHEN AN HOUR had passed and Eve was still pounding the treadmill as though she was carrying a message from the battlefield, Dom made her stop.

"Shower, then come eat," he urged her. He didn't have much appetite himself so he wasn't surprised when she only picked at the beautiful meal she'd arranged for her parents.

"Eve," he tried again as he topped up her wineglass.

"I don't want to talk." Her hollow-eyed gaze met his. "I'm going to pull a Dom and ignore my emotions, okay?"

He prided himself on keeping his emotions on the surface, rarely feeling anything at a deep level, but that rang through him with the agony of a broken bone.

He kept hearing her say, *I love Dom. I have since the first time we met.*

That seemed impossible. It made him angry because... He didn't know why it tripped his wires. Guilt? Because it made him feel as though he fell short? Or because he didn't believe her?

Evie didn't lie to him.

But she couldn't love him. Why would she? His heart

was as empty as his father's and his father's father. If he was lovable, his life would have been different.

Wouldn't it?

When Eve went to bed, he came into the bedroom with her.

"Not tonight, okay?" Eve flashed him a glance as she hurried to put on silk pajamas. "I—"

"I just want to hold you, Evie." It was the rawest, most needy thing he'd ever said.

After a charged moment, she nodded jerkily.

A few minutes later, they were in the dark, under the covers. She curled into his chest as he drew her into him. He felt all her hurt radiate out of her and soak into him. It was hellish, especially when he realized the small shudders rolling through her were sobs.

Every breath he took burned his lungs. He had never felt so helpless in his life, but he cuddled and coddled her, so damned grateful that she let him pet her and kiss her hair, and said, "Shh. We'll get through this. I promise."

He didn't know how, though. That kept him wide awake most of the night, long after she finally relaxed into sleep.

He lurched awake when he realized she was up and dressed in skinny jeans and a cable-knit pullover. She was brushing her hair and fastening it into a low ponytail.

"Where are you going?" He came up on an elbow.

"To sit with Mom at the hospital," she reminded him.

"Eve—I know you don't want to talk. I don't know what to say," he admitted, sitting up. "I hope you know that I care about you. I don't want to disappoint you. I want you to be happy in this marriage."

"I know. It's okay, Dom. It really is." She sat on the bench at the foot of the bed with her back to him as she zipped knee-high boots over her jeans. "I just find it hypocritical of Dad to worry about whether you love me when he and Mom didn't marry for love. They care about each other a lot, I know they do. It's the same way you care about my well-being so Dad knows that's not a bad reason to marry. It has served them really well and gave us a stable, privileged upbringing. I don't have anything to complain about. I'm lucky to have what they have. I know that."

Was she trying to convince herself? Because he felt sick at how bland that sounded. It sounded as though he was forcing her to settle when one of the things that made Evie the amazing woman she was, was her belief in herself and her own worth.

"You said yourself that I want to believe love is magic and can cure anything. You're right. I do. And I know that's unrealistic. I don't expect you to love me, Dom. I don't expect anything more from you than what we already have." She rose.

"I'll come have breakfast with you." He started to throw off the covers.

"I'll get something later. And you have that meeting with the London team. I'll text you once I have news."

By the time he was dressed and down the stairs, she was already gone.

Damn it.

He was pacing restlessly, wondering if he should go

to the hospital, when his doorman rang to say that Astrid was downstairs.

"Is everything all right?" he asked as she came off the elevator with Adio in her arms. They both wore speckles of rain and big smiles.

Astrid's cheerfulness quickly faded. "Is this a bad time? I was going to text from the pediatrician's, to make sure Eve still wanted to have coffee, but—"

"She probably forgot." Dom took the baby because he was kicking off his boots. He set the boy on his socked feet and took his wet jacket, following him as he took off into the lounge. "Eve's parents are back from their trip and her father had a procedure at the hospital today. She's gone to sit with her mother, to wait for news."

"Why aren't you with her?" Astrid asked, pausing in hanging up her own coat.

"She's angry with me. I didn't think she'd want me there."

"Dom." She clunked the hanger onto the rung. "You go anyway. That's how she knows it doesn't matter if she's angry, you'll always be there for her. What happened?"

"I—"

Don't want to talk about it.

He didn't. But he kind of did.

Adio had found the piano and was walking his hands across the keys, releasing discordant notes.

"Evie said you said our childhood was dysfunctional."

"Am I wrong?" she asked.

"Honestly, Astrid? How the hell would I know?" he asked with latent frustration. Maybe some unrecognized pain. "I wasn't there." He moved a vase of flowers off the coffee table and set it where Adio couldn't reach it. "My childhood didn't look that different from the rest of the boys at school. Plenty of them had parents who were divorced so…"

"My parents were married," she said gently. "It was still a train wreck."

"I know." He scratched his eyebrow. "Have you ever talked to anyone about it? Like, a professional?"

"Weekly, for the last eight years." Her tone was blunt as a hammer. "Do you want her number?"

"Maybe." He wanted to be more for Evie. Not just that weak sauce version of a marriage where he gave her stability and a few babies. He wanted—"Eve wants us to be like you and Jevaun."

He half expected her to laugh at him, but her brow crinkled in concern. "Do you love her?"

That sense of being on a diving board hit him again, only this time he was on the edge of a towering cliff, waves crashing into razor-sharp rocks below.

He drew a breath that felt like fire. "I don't even know what love is."

"Yes, you do," she said with a throb of despondency in her voice. "It's that thing we wanted from Dad and never got. That sense that it's okay to be vulnerable. I know it's scary to feel that way, Dom. But how do you think she feels if you don't love her? She's carrying around that same sense of not measuring up."

The pain that hit his chest was so visceral and sharp, Dom tried to rub it away with the heel of his hand. He couldn't stand for Eve to feel that cold and hollow. He would do anything to spare her. *Anything*.

"Pool?" Adio said, stretching to try to reach the latch.

Dom absently picked him up and said, "It's too cold for swimming." He opened the door so the wind gusted into their faces.

Adio cuddled into his shoulder. "Brr."

"Brr," Dom repeated. "That's right." He closed the door and rubbed the boy's narrow back. "Come visit when it's summer. Then we'll swim. Right now, I have to go see Auntie Evie."

"Abby Ebie."

"Exactly. Go put your boots on." He set the boy on his feet and Adio toddled to his boots.

"Thanks, Astrid." He could hardly look at her, finding that expression on her face too knowing, as though she saw all the way through him.

"Oh, you." She hurried across and hugged him.

He wrapped his arms around her shoulders and squeezed, compressing the abraded sensations in his chest, but when he released her, they weren't as bad as they'd been.

"It's like hugging a balloon animal," he said to cover how thin-skinned he felt.

"I dare you to say that to Eve once she's pregnant."

A stab of wistfulness pierced his chest. Would she still want that? Now that he understood how badly he'd hurt her, he didn't know how he'd make it up to her.

"I really like her, you know," Astrid said as she helped Adio with his jacket. "I can't help thinking you two were supposed to happen. Like it was fate or something."

"You know you sound like a hippie when you talk like that?" He held her coat for her. "But I think that's one of your most lovable qualities," he added, squeezing her shoulders.

"Nice save." She turned to face him. "Let me know how it goes, okay?"

"I will." Then he did the unthinkable and took the initiative to hug her again.

"What are you doing here?" Eve's heart lurched as Dom walked into the private waiting lounge at the hospital. "I thought you had a video chat with the team in London this morning?"

"I rescheduled. And brought brunch." He began unpacking the two cloth bags onto the small dining table, setting out pastries, yogurt parfaits and egg sandwiches.

"That was thoughtful of you." Ginny took a parfait and a spoon. "Thank you."

"I'll have one in a little while, thanks," Eve said, shaking her head when he offered one. She didn't mention there were ample meals available at the press of a button. This hospital catered to very wealthy patients. They ensured the comfort of families and caregivers during times of duress. "You don't have to stay," she added as he took off his overcoat. "It will be at least another hour, maybe two."

"I'd like to." He left his coat on a hook by the door. "Unless you'd rather I didn't?" His expression shuttered.

"No, you can if you want to. It's just that..." She hadn't expected this of him. She was incredibly touched and searched his eyes, wondering what had prompted this. Basic decency? Or something more?

The longer she looked into his whiskey-colored eyes, the more her heart felt pinched.

"Oh. Right." She remembered as Jackson walked in and came up short at the sight of Dom. "My brothers are coming."

"Traffic was terrible," Nico said as he came in behind Jackson and stepped around him. He nodded at them, then asked their mother, "Any news?"

"Not yet. Where's Christo?" Ginny set aside her parfait and stood.

"Chatting up a nurse, where do you think?" Nico kissed her cheek then came to peruse the food.

Jackson hadn't moved or spoken. In looks, he was a clone of Nico with more polish and style. Where Nico stuck to never-fail basics like a well-tailored, three-piece suit, Jackson wore things like striped trousers and chunky cardigans over a blue pullover and a winter scarf. They all would have teased him endlessly over his love of fashion if he didn't always look so effortlessly sophisticated.

He was still holding Dom's stare. Dom hadn't moved, either. Not one blink.

"Jackson." Ginny approached him. "It's good to see you."

"You too, Mom." He had to break the stare first to kiss her cheek, then lifted his head to say to Dom, "Let's go outside and talk."

"Oh, grow up," Eve muttered. "I married Dom to end the feud, not start a fresh one."

Christo came in wearing a fawn-colored coat over a black turtleneck and jeans. He frowned at Dom. "What are you doing here?"

"He's being a supportive husband." Eve was embarrassed by how rude they were.

"Is that what you're calling him? I thought this was a strategic alliance." Jackson curled his lip at Nico, apparently not confining his disgust to Dom and Eve.

"Maybe that is all I am to him," Eve said starkly, stepping forward to get in Jackson's face. "That's better than being his enemy. And maybe one of you could have 'made a strategic alliance' by now, instead of clinging to bachelorhood like you're Peter Pan and don't have any responsibilities to this family yourself."

They all had the grace to look away while Ginny said, "Eve, please. Can we have some peace while we're here?"

"Eve is more than a strategic alliance to me." Dom set the weight of his hands on her shoulders. His steady presence became a bolstering wall at her back. "If you want to hate me for marrying her, go ahead, but don't take it out on her. Not when Eve is creating peace for all of us. For me."

He squeezed her shoulders and she looked up, moved by the depth of emotion she found in his eyes. His expression was so tender, her heart swooped.

"When I'm with you, the battle stops. Everything inside me settles. That's worth everything to me."

Because he felt safe? Loved? The pinch in her heart clenched harder, but it felt oddly good, too. It wasn't being compressed. It was breaking past a thin shell, opening like a flower.

She covered one of the hands on her shoulder.

"You're acting like I'm asking you to surrender." Dom lifted his gaze to her brothers. "This marriage is a truce. Accept it."

"I have," Nico said gravely. "And I appreciate what you've done, Lina. Really. We *all* appreciate it," he said with a significant glower at her brothers.

Christo rolled his eyes and Jackson gave a discontented shrug as they both offered their hands.

"Congratulations on your marriage," Christo said.

"Look after her," Jackson added.

"I intend to," Dom vowed with such sincerity, hot tears of hope pressed behind her eyes.

"Dad was upset he didn't get to walk me down the aisle," Eve told Dom when they arrived back at the penthouse. "At least, that's what he said. He was pretty loopy from the anesthetic, but I think it was true."

She hoped it was also true that he loved her and only wanted her to be happy. She'd shed tears of relief all the way home because she thought he must be speaking from the heart, without his normal filter, and it gave her so much hope.

Dom took her coat, not saying anything.

Her glow of optimism dimmed. With her father's procedure successful and out of the way, their conflict from last night returned to sit between them like a coiled rattlesnake.

"Eve—"

"No, Dom, look. I'm fine. Honestly. I was upset last night because of the way Dad reacted. You've never lied to me about how you feel and—"

"You said you loved me from the first time we met," he interjected. "Why didn't you tell me sooner? Why did you tell your father instead of me?"

"Because—Because I didn't want to push you into saying something you don't feel. And because you make me feel raw and naked and like I'm waiting for you to notice me and want me and like me. Thank you for saying what you did at the hospital. It goes a long way, it really does, but can you at least show me a little pity? It's *hard* to love you."

He drew a sharp breath, head jerking back.

"Not because you're hard to love," she rushed to clarify. "You're so easy to love, Dom. You deserve to be loved. That's something I knew in here before I knew up here." She tapped her chest, then her temple. "I was so caught up in the feud, I didn't know I was falling for you. I only knew I shouldn't feel anything toward you except hatred. I knew that's all you felt toward me and that hurt, Dom. You don't know what it's like to love someone who resents you and—"

"Do I not?" he shot back. His voice wasn't loud, but it was so powerful, she felt it like thunder in her chest.

"W-what?"

"I didn't know what it was, either. How could I? I've never felt it. Yes, there was some weak version of it from my mother and my sisters, but it was drowned out by my father's nastiness and Ingrid's spite. All I knew was that I'd met a woman who was some kind of supercharged metal and I was a magnet that couldn't stay away. God, Evie." He ran his hand down his face. "It was hell to be apart from you. When I left you in Australia, I thought I was going to be sick. I tried to hate you, I did, but I couldn't even work up hatred for your family anymore. I just wanted you, damn it. I *need* you. I know that doesn't make sense, but…"

"It makes sense. I feel that way, too. So what is the 'but'?" She came close enough to pick up his hands. She held them close in the nook of her neck while she searched the tortured amber of his eyes. "I'm not trying to hurt you by making you say anything you don't feel, Dom. But I want to show you that it's okay. That I'm right here and it's safe. We have each other's back. We don't lie to each other. If you say it, I'm going to believe you and we are going to be stronger than we ever thought possible."

Her lips were quivering so hard, it was hard to talk. This was a huge chance on her part to say that. She was reaching for the thing she had always wanted and clenched her hands tighter on his, feeling as though she might shatter if this didn't go the way she hoped. But she needed all of him. Not the muffled, opaque shell, but the man inside. His heart.

"How is it so terrifying to say when it doesn't even express what I feel? I do love you, Evie." He flinched as though bracing for a blow, but a sudden brightness entered his gaze. His expression turned tender and a slow smile began to pull at his lips. "I didn't know it would feel like that. I love you so hard I'm afraid I'll break you with it."

"Impossible." She released his hands and stepped into his arms, lifting her lips. "Our love is the healing kind. The kind that ends wars and builds kingdoms and changes history."

"You're changing *me*," he said as his mouth found hers. "I feel good. Hopeful."

"Loved?"

"Yes." His damp gaze met hers very briefly before he closed his eyes.

She cradled his face, allowing that small shield because this was new and delicate and deserved to be treated gently. She pressed her mouth to his, whispering, "It's okay. We don't have to talk right now. We can show each other how we feel."

He groaned and pulled her into a strong embrace. His kiss deepened, but stayed reverent and so imbued with emotion, she felt tears dampen her lashes.

They shed their clothes between kisses on the way to their bedroom, sliding between the sheets while gray skies hung low and fall rains gusted against the windows. They sheltered each other and warmed skin with hot kisses and kindled passion with the brush of thigh to thigh, belly to belly, chest to chest. They kissed soft and sweet and long and deep and then the flames caught for real, the way they always did, engulfing them in a bonfire that would burn them to ashes so they could arise anew.

When his body joined with hers, they both groaned in relief and stared in wonder at the other. She caressed his cheek and he brushed her hair off her brow and set a tender kiss there.

"Do you think we were destined to meet?" she asked him.

"Maybe it was just a very lucky coincidence. More than one."

"Despite the odds."

"Exactly." He withdrew and returned, making them both shake.

"It's so good."

"I know. Always." He did it again and her eyelids fluttered in pleasure.

He made a gratified noise. "Are you going to shatter for me, Evie? And let me watch you and feel it and know I give you this?"

A latent pang of exposure struck, but it faded as quickly as it arrived. She had no need to feel threatened by him. By this. Of all the places in the world, she was safest when she was in his arms.

"Yes," she said on a languid groan, nibbling his chin. "I have no secrets from you. No defenses left."

Emotions flickered across his face—satisfaction and tenderness and acknowledgment of the daunting power he held over her.

He slid his fingertip along her bottom lip and said, "Then you'll do the same to me, because you're my perfect match in every way, aren't you?"

"I am and I will," she promised as she ran her hand into his hair and brought his mouth down to his, urging him with the tilt of her hips to take her to paradise.

He did.

EPILOGUE

Two years later...

EVE HAD A lot of sympathy for Nonna Maria these days. Astrid and her four children had left yesterday and she was still sweeping sand out of the kitchen.

"He needs a top-up before he goes to bed," Dom said, coming in with Oliver.

Their three-month-old son was pushing one little arm against Dom's shoulder. The other fist was in his mouth. He was gumming it vigorously, but he squawked when he caught sight of her.

"He had a really big diaper and a really big burp, then he turned into a lamprey when he found the skin on my arm. I'll finish that." He took the broom as she took the baby.

"Are you having a growth spurt?" she asked her son as she rubbed her nose to his. She was drowning in so much love for him, and the husband who watched her with such an indulgent look on his face, it was silly.

The September evening was mild and the sky was painted every shade from gold to rose to indigo. She stepped outside to sit on the swing and kick it into motion while she nursed. Oliver got down to business straightaway, but he was ready for bed so his eyelids began to droop very quickly.

She breathed the fresh air, soaking up this perfect moment because they were heading back to New York in a few days and even though she was technically on maternity leave, she was still very involved with all the structural changes Dom and Nico were implementing.

"It's our anniversary tomorrow," she said when Dom sat down and stretched his arm behind her.

"You keep saying you have baby brain, but you do know it's not April, don't you? There were tulips in the park when we had our photos done, remember?"

How could she forget? Their wedding reception had turned into five hundred guests witnessing them renew their vows. She'd worn an extravagant gown as Romeo had walked her down the aisle. Her mother had shed happy tears in the front row and Maya had been in seventh heaven as the flower girl. Even Ingrid had said a few kind words when all the toasts were made, right before they cut into the five-tiered cake.

The feud was over and everyone had turned out to celebrate that fact.

"Not our third anniversary," she chided him. "Our second. Our first was Budapest…"

"Oh. Now I'm embarrassed." He showed her an empty hand. "I didn't get you anything to mark the occasion."

"You can make it up to me once he's down for the night."

"Oh?" A slow smile crept across his lip and his voice

dipped into that sexy one that made her tingle all over. "How do you suggest I do that?"

"I was thinking we could play 'stranded on a tropical island.'"

"Evie Blackwood," he said in a mock outrage. "You are a woman after my own heart, aren't you?"

"I thought it was already mine?"

"It absolutely is," he assured her warmly as he nuzzled his lips into her neck.

* * * * *

If you couldn't put down Marrying The Enemy *then why not dive into these dramatic other stories by Dani Collins?*

A Baby To Make Her His Bride
Awakened On Her Royal Wedding Night
The Baby His Secretary Carries
The Secret Of Their Billion-Dollar Baby
Her Billion-Dollar Bump

Available now!